# WISHMASTER

## THE NOVELIZATION

## CHRISTIAN FRANCIS

Encyclopocalypse Publications
www.encyclopocalypse.com

# FOREWORD

MARK ALAN MILLER

What is a wish? A desire of the heart. An utterance of the soul. The yearning of our deepest, darkest fantasies to be brought to glorious life. To wish is to be human. To grant wishes is divine.

Or is it?

That is the question begged by Peter Atkins. Peter's contributions to movies, and the written word have cemented his position as a horror icon. And, having had the pleasure of working together in close quarters, I can say with certainty that the man is a genius.

This is exactly what a movie that could have been a forgettable foray into the 'killer genie' sub-genre has, decades after its release, become a fan favorite horror classic that receives constant tributes in the form of retrospective articles, screenings, and special edition home video releases packed with bonus features.

What's the secret behind its staying power? Maybe it's' because Pete asks the question, "Why is it that our wishes can't be granted? What manner of beast would wield such power? And how could this beast exist without becoming the embodiment of pure evil?"

Thus, the Djinn as we now know him, was born. When he was set loose upon the screen, he joined our world, grabbed firmly onto our consciousness, and has never let go.

While countless horror films have been released and summarily forgotten, *Wishmaster* gave glorious life to 3 sequels, a stage play, an action figure, and legions of fans that have remained loyal to the franchise since day one.

Now it is time for the Djinn to conquer yet another aspect of the cultural consciousness: that of the novel.

That brings us to Christian Francis, the author of the novel you are about to read. Christian understands every aspect of his role in this endeavor. If you've read his other works, you'll know why he was chosen for the job. Christian works with archetypes like a deranged puppeteer, and he plays with story the way a magician does a deck of cards.

This isn't a passing of the torch. This is a keeping of the flame.

Christian Francis and Peter Atkins are two of my favorite people on this planet. I love their imaginations, and I cannot describe the joy I feel when I get to watch their minds at work.

With their powers now combined, a journey unlike any other lies beyond these words.

If you're reading this, it means you asked for it.

And as they say...be careful what you wish for.

Mark Alan Miller
January 2021

*Listen well, O best beloved,*
*for these are the words of the wise.*
*Once, in a time before time,*
*God saw three things.*
*He saw light. He saw earth. He saw fire.*
*And God breathed into each*
*and to each his breath was life.*
*And the light gave birth to Angels.*
*And the earth gave birth to Men.*
*And the fire gave birth to the Djinn.*
*And the Children of Light were given heaven as a home.*
*And the Children of the Earth were given a home which is this*
*world.*
*Only the Children of Fire were homeless, doomed to wander*
*between worlds, belonging to neither and envious of each.*
*Fear not the teeth of the leopard, O best beloved.*
*Fear not the roar of the thunder.*
*For this world has no perils to compare to the rage of these*
*Orphans of God.*
*Fear one thing only in all that is.*
*Fear the Djinn.*

# PROLOGUE

PERSIA - 1122AD

Today was a new day in the court of the Persian King. Revelers sat along both sides of the banquet table that ran the length of the expansive sandstone throne-room. Though adorned with a tablecloth of such luxury and bejeweled with the finest gems, it paled in comparison to the rest of the decor's opulence. Atop the table sat the food they ate and the wine they drank. Only the *most* exquisite, only the rarest.

Along the walls of this room were draped the finest and most colorful cottons and silks. Each hung like flags without any wind, positioned equidistantly in between dozens of jewel-encrusted golden bowls which rested on high, circular, marble plinths. In each bowl sat a bright flame, which, as one, cast a brilliant glow around this royal chamber, pushing away any lurking darkness.

High above the banquet sat the vaulted ceiling: as impressive as it was decadent. Each beam had been decorated with intricate carvings that depicted the long and colorful history of this land.

Each one of the dozens upon dozens of revelers toasted their ruler's name with every sip of wine that passed their lips. And each time they did so, the king - fat and corrupt upon his throne - grimaced with contempt at them.

Yesterday, this could never have happened.

Yesterday, the king was to have been introduced to the executioner's scimitar.

But that fate changed when the king called forth a creature of immense power.

Yesterday, the king *thought* he wanted this slavering celebration.

He'd thought it far preferable than the everlasting death to which he had been sentenced.

But *these* people.

*This* adulation.

This wasn't what he'd asked for. Not exactly. Surely his new friend understood that?

For depravity was what the king had desired. He wanted to sit on his throne at the end of this room and watch his subjects debase themselves, solely for his pleasure, as they sang songs of his name. He wanted to see their flesh combining. He wanted to see their carnal revelry. He wanted to smell the forbidden juices of those who had devoted their lives to him, all while they screamed his glories with every ecstatic arrival. Yet, even as a king, a man whose words were that of a god to his people, he was too cautious to offer a word of correction for his new friend. So, instead of demanding a change, he sat on his throne watching his court. Watched them eat, drink and praise him in ways that were profoundly pedestrian.

"I'm bored," said the king, his voice barely a whisper.

Dressed in a long, hooded black robe, a figure stood beside the king's golden throne. It turned to the King, its movements bordering on serpentine. "My master..." Its voice was guttural and wicked, though the words it spoke had barely any trace of the contempt and hatred which hid behind each and every syllable. "Was this not your wish? Did I not give you back the love of your masses?"

With its face embraced by shadow, this figure's chin remained barely visible despite the abundance of flames which leaped from the bowls scattered about the hall, as if this figure itself created its own darkness that cowered within the thick hessian garments it wore.

"Did you not ask for this?" With each new word, a grin crawled up this figure's cheeks. "To be... praised once more?"

"*This* is not my desire..." the king grumbled as he heard yet *another* toast of his name.

"Then... what is your second wish?"

The king looked up to the hooded figure. How had this happened? How had his luck changed so fast? *This Angel may look like a Devil,* he thought, *but he is* mine *to command.*

The king glanced for a moment to either side of him - at the eight guards who stood stoic, to protect him. Though now it felt like they were here to keep him prisoner; trapped in the manacles of banality - just as they'd kept him prisoner only the day before.

"I wish my court to be more... entertaining than this."

Like a gift to its ears, the hooded figure could no longer contain its glee. A low, sickly laugh escaped its lips as it turned toward the court.

"As you wish..." it said.

In the passing of a few beats of the king's heart, this gathering of royal subjects who had been feasting in luxury, now became indeed more entertaining. But not for the king.

Nor for any man or woman occupying the room. The robed figure was the only creature here that would or could be entertained by the impending atrocities.

As if awakened into a nightmare vision of violence and chaos, the veil of this serene banquet instantly transformed into a new, hellish vision - a vision filled with death and a thousand screams.

The same revelers remained, but they were no longer merry with the contentment of their feast - instead they were brimming with a raw, primal panic. Now, upon their feet, they rushed in search of any escape they could find, all headed to the only exit; the large doors at the opposite end of the room. None of them stopped for a moment to consider their bewildering adulation toward their ruler. The truth of it was, this adulation had only been their reality for a couple of hours. But their recent past was little more than a distant dream, wiped clean by the magic of the robed figure's command. And, like that dream of their previous hatred for their king, the memory of this recent celebratory banquet had now also disappeared. All they knew, as the king looked upon them in terror, was the horrifying reality of their certain and imminent demise.

As the men, women and children fled from the large room and ran down the long corridor that led to the palace courtyard, one man strode inward with a determined expression on his elderly face. Against this tide of panic filling the large corridor, the old man barged his way through their screams and flailing limbs. This was the Court Sorcerer, Zoroaster. He had served multiple kings, but none had been as foolish as the one who sat now upon the throne. Zoroaster had served cruel men, greedy men, ignorant men, but never one so weak and impudent as the one that currently claimed the crown.

From among the stream of people escaping, as if picked up by an unseen hand, a screaming man was ripped from Zoroaster's path. The man's body was thrown across the corridor, slamming with an almighty force against the wall. His bones splintered as he collided with the stone.

Instead of sliding to the floor to bleed out slowly, for that is what fate *would* have dictated in any traditional reality, his body remained stuck in the same crumpled position, six feet off the floor. The man's body disobeyed gravity, and the agony continued as he tried to breathe, tried to move, tried to do anything to escape this sudden hell. Before any scream could escape from his lungs, however, every one of his organs succumbed to a fate he knew to be his death. Though he was correct that death was waiting in the wings, this feeling inside was *not* the feeling of the actual end of his life, but rather the feeling of the *cause* of the end of his life. A fierce chill spread through his body. A heavy coldness that matched the very sandstone from which he was unable to fall. The last moments of this poor soul's life were consumed with a fear he had never thought possible, as he witnessed his skin harden and pale to the same hue as the rock of which he was quickly becoming a part. As the stone consumed the flesh of his heart, it strangled the last drops of life away from him. His sight finally clouded and extinguished a second later.

Though by now he was dead, the transformation of his body continued until every part of him had turned to stone; until he had become like a grotesque bas-relief carved by some lunatic sculptor; hanging theatre as much a part of the corridor as the very of which stone he was now made. Among the twisted limbs, his face sat still - frozen in its final screaming torment. This happened in barely any time at all - while most of the revelers still tried to flee. This torturous fate was not an isolated incident, however. No. More were to become part of the bastardized wish of the idiot king.

The first man to exit the corridor into the courtyard had thought himself safe. But he was caught in a similarly impossible execution to his sandstone countryman. The moment his foot hit the courtyard floor, his nerves shredded into an agonizing strain as the flesh on his stomach ripped itself apart. His legs buckled, and he fell to his knees. The tear on his belly - which opened as though torn by invisible hands- created a wound which cut wide across him and curled up like a lascivious smile.

Among the gushing blood that spilled out onto the floor, his intestines tumbled out of him like a tongue. But before they could land on the sandy ground, one part ripped away from the entrance to his bowel, turned upward, and slithered back up his body of its own accord. It moved up his body with great speed, like a gore-soaked snake somehow woken from its slumber by a demonic charmer's pipe.

Glistening wetly, it wrapped itself around the man's throat, then shot further up, reaching high toward one of the corridor's ceiling beams, which rested over thirty feet up. The rope of gut grabbed the beam, and hauled itself backward. The man's body was yanked from the floor - where his blood had been pooling around him - high into the air as his futile screams were choked. His murderous innards had become his own personal hangman. Still full of the food he had eaten only minutes before, his intestines undulated as if still trying to digest their contents. The remaining blood fell from within, spilling from his open cavity like crimson rain, dripping onto the escaping crowd below.

As Zoroaster fought to make his way to the throne room, the blood from above fell onto him too. Lifting his arm to shield himself, he managed to glance at the hanged body swinging from its guts. Then, before the sorcerer could even look away, a woman barged past him, her arm striking him in the face as she flailed wildly. Her screams were especially piercing and full of an agony that caused it to be heard above many of the other moans and wails.

She grabbed Zoroaster, but as she did, he witnessed her long brown hair suddenly escape the confines of her headdress and begin to burrow itself into her face, penetrating her flesh wherever her skin had been on show; each strand of this hair like a needle and thread which started to sew up her eyes, her mouth, and her nose. The threads pulling themselves so taut that her screams could no longer escape past her lips. The strands then worked their way through her lips, pierced her gums and teeth, and stitched their way down her throat to consume her voice box, and finally moved onto her lungs. Choking, she collapsed at the sorcerer's feet. A mute mass killed by the abuse of her own sentient pelt.

Zoroaster, his eyes filled with fear, anger, and sorrow, resumed his path to the room ahead, where the king sat on his ill-deserved throne. Zoroaster realized that he could not help any of the people dying around him. His quarry was the cause of all of this, and there was nothing he could do to help these casualties of the king's wishes. With steely determination, Zoroaster had to remind himself that *he* was a sorcerer. His powers were far greater than those who succumbed to the abuse of the disgusting evil. So he had to fight the root of the problem to vanquish this evil - then, after, he would deal with the king, too.

In every direction, those who attempted escape met with a fate worse than simple death. Their screams combined to make a cacophonous death cry that drowned out the sounds of their stampede. None of these victims were punished the same. Each met their own terrible end, conjured by the terrible depths of the creature in the robes.

A woman had collapsed at the side of the corridor, with her head, hands, and feet mutated from flesh into some gnarled wood. Like the man in the stone wall, her body had given itself up to a new state of being. Her body abandoned its fleshy humanity for a wooden existence. As she moaned, long branches burst from her torso - out and upwards - and upon each branch, hellishly beautiful blood-red flowers blossomed at speed.

The escaping hordes soon trampled her, too. These people blindly fled, breaking her branches under their sandals as they did so. Her new wooden countenance had been born, and then destroyed in less than a minute.

A small boy followed, screaming, his arms held up in front of him. His hands had broken apart and fused back together into a nightmarish configuration within seconds. Each fist had mutated into the head of what seemed a giant angry toad, complete with sickening tongues, flicking out in shows of territorial aggression. They had been looking forward, until without any cause, they suddenly turned their attention back toward the boy. Their serrated teeth on full display as they roared at him, ready to attack their one-time master.

All sought freedom, but the only thing they found was punishment. Some were bloodied, some transformed, some had bodies which turned against them, but none made it to the safety of the desert outside. None even made it more than a few steps into the courtyard.

Near the door to the throne-room, a man - his body twitching and pulsing as if it contained something that sought freedom - grabbed at Zoroaster's arm.

"Help me, sorcerer! Help me!" the man yelled.

But Zoroaster could not stop. He yanked himself out of the man's grip and continued ahead.

Half-collapsed, the condemned man screamed and gasped for air. His mouth opened wider and wider, until his lips tore at their edges; ripping open as his skull forced its way out from its fleshy shell, shedding its skin until the whole skeleton had scrambled out. Once it cleared its bones several feet from the mass of gore, it quickly fell, lifeless, to the ground.

Finally drawing close to the throne-room, Zoroaster witnessed a group of five fleeing people crash into each other as if they were marionettes under another's control; picked off their feet by something unseen and smashed together. As they collided, their flesh quickly broke through their clothing, stretching out and flowing from their bodies, melting together. Before the sorcerer could make sense of the scene in front of him, the five beings became one mass of flesh, bone, and torment; a thing of glistening, mutated flesh, mottled in blood and studded with random body parts. To Zoroaster's horror, it still somehow moved toward him - crawling along with the flow of those also attempting to escape - every sliding step it took, a step of agony. Behind it was an oily trail of bloody mucus - a pitiful creature no better than a snail torn free from its shell.

Making his way around the monstrosity, the sorcerer at last arrived at the entrance to the throne-room. Before him stood the archway that led to the evil inside. Coming to a stop, he paused for a brief moment to steady his nerves.

From within the shadows beside him, a hand suddenly flew out and grabbed the sorcerer's ankle. Another victim begging for assistance. Looking down with a cry of shock, Zoroaster saw a man who had been half-transformed into a giant snake. Through his broken face, this snake man gurgled at the sorcerer, "Free us, wizard! Lift this curse. Help us!"

Jerking free, Zoroaster entered the room, which only minutes ago had been a bright and shining room of decadence - a jewel of the palace. But now the room he entered was seemingly composed solely of darkness. Given over to torment.

The sounds of those trying to escape could be heard behind him. Screams of the damned. The breaking of bones. The tearing of skin. All echoed and combined to make a noise no human ears should ever have to hear.

Lined up before the throne stood eight stone soldiers, four on each side. These were the remnants of the royal guard, caught unaware by a magic which had grabbed their souls and twisted their beings to a new, dark reality. Now, they were frozen in place like the honor guard to the king of death and torture; their final poses held in varying stages of attack. Some had swords half-unsheathed, others were in mid-strike. All were stone. All damned. Around them lay the splintered remnants of the banquet table, and what was left of the food, crushed underfoot from the escaping revelers.

Blanketed by a thick shadow, the king sat on his throne, aghast and gibbering in horror at what has been done to his people.

"No..." he said, under his breath. He turned with disgust at the hooded figure who now towered over him. The thing had seemingly grown taller than before, his features almost one with the darkness of the room. "By the name of God! This isn't what I wanted," the king said. He wept in torment.

"Then," the figure replied, "wish it away, exalted one. Wish it all away..."

Without breaking his stride, and before the king could

reply, Zoroaster rushed in front of him. "Stop! Stop! No more wishes!"

The dark, hooded figure turned to the sorcerer. Its shadowed grin vanished. As it snarled at the man now shouting at the king.

"I beg your majesty. *Silence*!" Zoroaster shouted.

His soul in despair, the king looked to his sorcerer, the fall of his world finally breaking through his myopia. But what could he do now? After all, what was a king to this god... this Devil? He only had one choice. To wish them safe. To stop his selfishness.

"My poor people." The king's voice was weak, yet resolute, "I must..."

"Do you wish their fate on all the world?" Zoroaster said. "No more wishes! No more words!"

The dark figure took a step toward Zoroaster, its voice low, full of the promise of death. "I warn you, wizard. Hold your tongue. Or I shall hold it for you."

The sorcerer ignored these words, remaining focused on the king. "One more wish is all this vile creature needs. Three wishes granted, to he who woke it, lets it open the gateway to the *void*. The gateway between worlds."

"New wonders, majesty. New splendors," the figure said, bending down closer to the king, its tone approximating sincerity.

"And new, terrible masters!" Zoroaster shouted at the king. His contemptuous gaze moved to the disgusting creature at his king's side.

The king looked helplessly from Zoroaster to the figure, then back again.

The figure, aggravated at the appearance of this magician, but not allowing him to slow down its plan, looked around the room, and smiled at what was arriving. Throughout the lofty spaces of the throne-room, reality started to shimmer, as it lost its stability entirely. The inscrutable movements of great and awful shapes could be seen whirling in the furthest, blackest corners of the room. Demonic whispers filled the air. Monstrous forces had gathered eagerly at the border between this and another world.

The king glared up at this threat, realizing that Zoroaster was right, that he could not take the path offered by this figure. So, at last, he spoke with certainty. "No! By all that's holy!"

"Zoroaster," The king pleaded, "do something!"

The sorcerer needed no prompting. He quickly reached within the folds of his robe and his hand emerged, clutching a fire-red opal. With his eyes closed, he started to recite an invocation.

The robed figure hastened its entreaty, offering more wicked promises. "Make the wish, my king. *Anything* your heart desires!"

"*No!*" the king said.

"My brethren will reward you with pleasures undreamed of by any man."

The king stared into the figure's corrupting eyes. He now saw the beast for what it was; a vile creation who offered nothing but condemnation and corruption.

"Wish!" the figure said, again. "Or your torment will be eternal!"

Zoroaster's hands did not remain idle. As the robed figure pressed the king, the sorcerer continued to work his spell. With all the ancient incantations he could summon, the opal soon rose from Zoroaster's palm and hovered a few inches in the air. "Nib shiggaath bahim! Nib shiggaath bahim!" he cried over and over, and the opal pulsed with a deep red light.

With a snarl, the figure turned from the king and saw the

gem in the sorcerer's hand. Its expression turned to shock. "*Impudent worm!*" it said. "*Thief!*"

The demonic whispers deep in the shadows reached fever pitch, quickly building into screams of pure fury, caused by the intensifying pain resulting from the sorcerer's spell. A pain that had somehow grabbed hold of this robed creature and sent agonies searing through its body. The beast screamed at Zoroaster, its voice booming with hatred. "*Your body will be dust as I feast on the bones of your ancestors!*"

These words echoed throughout the room and were soon ripped away from this reality and taken to another. Zoroaster's magic had silenced the evils the figure had wrought. The shapes in the all-consuming darkness, and the figure - all gone from the room, in an instant.

As a mark of completion, a blinding flash of white light erupted from within the opal - a shockwave of old power. For a brief moment, the light bled into every inch of the palace, across all rooms, extinguishing every shadow; cleansing all unholiness.

When the light had dissipated, the flames in the bowls around the throne room were again lit. Though the figure was expelled, its destruction remained. The revelers who had attempted to flee, remained all along the long corridor as felled corpses. Zoroaster stared back in pity at their remains. Then each bubbled into a strange transmuting matter, breaking down their beings into a collective puddle of gore and waste. He smiled, because he knew this was the effect of the corruption being expunged from them, causing each part of their remains to break down and shed the unholiness. When all had separated into pools of decay, at the place where each person had died, a growth impossibly blossomed upward; the last of the effects of the evil fighting to remain in this world. But it was an impossible battle, as the sorcerer's magic had already bested the demon. These growths resembled sculptures of large flowers, and as the swelling slowed, they ossified from blood, bone and flesh into a solid bright white stone. In a matter of moments, all along this corridor, the executed remnants now resembled pale orchids from the fields of the inferno. Cleansed and pure.

The hovering opal, still glowing and pulsing with a fierce red light, dropped back down into Zoroaster's hand. Its illumination slowly faded, until all that remained was a large gemstone.

A smile of victory crept over his face, and he lifted the gem up to the light. Staring fixedly upon the object, he saw something deeply troubling within.

"What have I done," said the king in a weak deflated voice.

Seething internally, Zoroaster chose not to reply. He would ensure that this pretender to the throne would pay for his crimes soon enough.

"Zoroaster," the king said. "Did you cast it from this land? Are we safe?"

"All innocence under the eyes of the creator can rest easy," the sorcerer replied, as he gazed about the devastation wrought by the presence of the demonic scourge, "For now."

# YOUR FIRST WISH

Do not presume that you read these words alone.

Did you think I would not be paying attention?

I am here with you, standing just beyond the veil of reality.

As your eye glanced upon this page, and as your mind thirsted for knowledge, you called me unto you.

Your want is as inevitable as the tide itself.

Your want is expected.

Your want is predictable.

This tale is not told for just anyone to hear, but only for those who crave it. Those who wish for it.

This is your last chance to walk away...

You remain?

You desire to know my story?

. . .

*As you wish...*

# Damnation Unleashed

# CHAPTER
# ONE



"Shit!" Josh Aickman said, as his body slammed onto the wooden floor of the squash court. "How do you keep beating me?"

His t-shirt twisted halfway up his torso, causing his pasty-white paunch to be on full display. The sweat dripped from him in a torrent, soaking through his clothes. He knew full well he looked as unfit as he felt.

He also knew why he never won this game. He could not admit aloud just how out of shape he was. He may have been only twenty-six years old, but he felt his body was that of a forty-year-old with the physical fitness of a bed-ridden pensioner. He could get away with that if he considered himself good-looking, but he certainly didn't feel that way about himself. So he subjected himself to this ritual humiliation on the squash court, and remained outwardly confused as to his losing streak.

He *wanted* to be the muscular type - but he was not. He *wanted* to be the chiseled-jaw athlete - but he was not. He *wanted* to be worthy of his opponent - but he *most definitely* was not.

His opponent was Alexandra Amberson.

His best friend was Alexandra Amberson.

Alexandra Amberson was also his angel. The woman he had silently been in love with since they were children. But it was never meant to be. So, they both carried on with their lives remaining on each other's radar at all times; always there as a shoulder for each other to lean on - and he was fine with that. Well, he *had* to be fine with it. If friendship was all she could give, then that was all he needed. Despite his hidden desires, he remained there for her platonically, as she was for him. It was even her idea to start this weekly assassination of his self-worth.

He told her he wanted to get in shape, yet he couldn't bring himself to sign up to a gym. So she offered to help. And, true to her word, she came here with him week in, week out - dragged him here on most occasions - and in every single session, she demolished him in an almost ritualistic flurry of amazing point domination that always sent him, running, out of breath, and collapsing, on a regular basis, all over the court. She never took it easy on him. Every time they played, she remained poised. Concentrated. Her hands, powerful. Her eyes, sharp. She was not here to take it easy on him.

"Guess that's it!" Alex said as she walked over to Josh, who remained slumped on the floor, the racquet laying on the ground a few feet away from his grip. His attempted display of skill ended up with him missing the ball by a clear yard, sending him crashing down to the floor via the wall. He would feel it the next morning, as he did the morning after every game.

"Guess it is," Josh replied. "Lemme guess, you went easy on me?"

Alex smiled *that* smile at him, the one that filled him with joy even though he *knew* it did not mean what he *hoped* it did.

Clambering to his feet, he pulled the sodden T-shirt back down over his stomach and followed Alex to the bench, as he slyly adored her slim physique. He was always surprised that her long brown hair looked as good after a game as before one. Her hair fell gracefully over her naturally beautiful face. One which needed no makeup.

"Good game," she said as she sat down and picked up her water bottle, taking a swig.

"If you say so. Jesus, I haven't beaten you at a game since college," he said, struggling to catch his breath. "And how the fuck aren't you sweating? Look at you! Not even a single drop!"

"Is this a male pride thing?" she snickered before offering her bottle to him.

Grabbing it, he took a gulp, and swallowed before replying. "No. It's much more personal than that. Besides, I haven't had pride since graduation."

Laughing loudly, Alex couldn't help but marvel at how easy their time was together. How much she loved him. He was like the best brother she could hope for.

"You talk to Nathan?" Josh asked as casually as he could muster. He knew Alex hated talking about her romantic relationships. He saw her stiffen a little at the question.

"No," she replied, as he handed her bottle back. "It's over for good."

"What's it been?" he asked. "All of six weeks?"

"Seven and a half."

Josh grabbed his bag from under the bench and sat down next to her. "Not like you're counting," he said as he took out his towel.

"What are you? My analyst?" Her words, though jocular, were tinged with a slight annoyance.

Trying to lighten up the subject, he retorted, "I *wish* I was your analyst! I could use the extra cash." Her smile at his joke made him breathe a little easier. He didn't want to upset her, but he found himself continuing without thinking. "It's just... I was thinking... you know..."

Alex smiled as they both stood and walked toward the exit. "Thinking what?"

"Well, maybe *we* should go out."

*Oh God,* Josh thought in a panic, *did I just ask that?*

Alex's smile faltered. An awkward moment. She knew what he meant, but she wished this wouldn't rear its head again. She hated to hurt him, and she *did* like him, but she wasn't ready for this. Not yet. She couldn't risk losing him for a stupid mistake, especially when she didn't really know what she wanted with her life. So she pretended not to know what he was talking about. To give him an out. She knew how panicked he must be - this was normally something he only proposed when black-out drunk.

"We go out all the time, Josh," she said, hoping he would take the option to escape.

Opening the door to the gym parking lot, Josh motioned for her to walk through - the perfect gentleman as always. A gentleman who was still sweating profusely, but from nerves at the moment, not physical exertion.

"Yeah, we go out. But we don't go *out, out.* You know what I mean?" As he spoke those words, Josh couldn't believe how brave he was being. He knew what her reply would be, but he had to make sure he wasn't missing an opportunity of a lifetime. She was single. So, now was a time as good as any, right? Not that she'd ever wanted to punch under her weight before with him, but maybe she had a secret fetish for sad, unfit, brother-type friends?

"You're my best friend. I... I don't want to lose that."

He tried to keep a brave face, but those words hurt him. Of course, he already knew how she felt, and he knew it was unfair of him to ask the question. He saw the hurt in her eyes at having to say no. She put a hand on his arm as they came to a stop, a few yards short of the parked cars.

"Josh, it isn't you. Really. You gotta believe me. It's me. All me. I've got too many issues. There's..." She paused for a beat as she tried to find the words, "I've been through some stuff. Stuff I never told you about. I need to get myself together first." She forced a smile. "Or, maybe it's just that Shannon's right about me? I'm a control freak, and can't deal with change?"

With the mention of Shannon's name, and the prospect of this getting more and more awkward, Josh gave up the fight and let them both off the hook.

"And how *is* your beautiful younger sister? She's happy with the job?"

*Thank you Josh*, Alex thought, relieved. "I *guess* she is. But her telling me that might sound too much like gratitude. And you know how she is."

Weirdness averted.

"Give her a break," Josh replied with a smile. "She's young. She's only been here, what, six months? She needs help settling in."

Walking on again, they approached their cars, which had been parked next to each other.

"Maybe you're right," she said. And then, absent-mindedly, "Hey, maybe you should take *her* out." Was this too much, too soon? She hoped not.

"I think I'm three tattoos and a nipple-ring short of the

ideal Shannon mate," Josh replied with a chuckle, which in turn made Alex laugh too; half from relief.

"That's true," she said, as she took her car keys from her pocket. "But you're real close to the ideal *Alex* male, and I don't want you thinking otherwise. No matter how crazy my brain is."

As he heard this, Josh took out his keys and opened his car trunk, putting his bag in. "So what do I need to be bang on target?"

"Patience."

Feeling the need to explain more, she continued, "I'm just... I don't know. Sometimes I just feel like I'm still waiting for my life to *mean* something, and I don't want you caught in the wake of my... stupidity."

Shutting the trunk, Josh unlocked his car door. "You and two billion others. It's called twentieth century anxiety. The true wonder of the modern age is that we all haven't collectively killed ourselves out of fear."

"You're such a philosopher, Josh."

"I very well could've been, but that wouldn't have paid the rent." He got into his car, and wound down the window, looking out at her as she opened her own car door. "Anyway, say 'Hi' to Shannon for me."

After they said their goodbyes, and Josh drove off, a plume of exhaust fumes from his decrepit vehicle smeared the air. Alex wondered whether he was angry with her for the pathetic explanation - yet again. But what *could* she do? She was a mess. She was a mess, and selfishly needed Josh there as only her friend. At least, for now.

The overpowering stench of gasoline and rotten fish permeated the breeze at one of the city's more questionable dockyards. From the early morning 'til way past the midnight hour, seven days a week, three hundred and sixty-five days a year, boats and ships of all kinds traveled through these harbors. From fishing trawlers to immense cargo haulers; if it *could* be imported through the docks, it *was*. Legal or illegal. As long as there was some manner of paperwork, the vessels were permitted to dock. Renting one of the dockside warehouses may have not been cheap, but they *were* private, and for the teams of stevedores who worked here, they blindly loaded and unloaded what they were told to. If they saw something, they didn't say anything - as long as there was a paycheck waiting for them, they kept their judgements to themselves. They just needed to keep their minds on the prize, and for most of the workers, their prize was to end each night with a beer or five in their hands, and a warm body to sleep next to.

As Anthony Beaumont stood on the dock side, waiting for his delivery, he certainly didn't care about the dockyard's reputation for not being entirely above board. All he cared about was his find: what was on the ship, now moored. That was it. That was *all*. At least it was for now, until he discovered the next priceless artifact he *had* to acquire. Then after that, there would be another, and another.

In front of the large, docked ship, Beaumont stood next to the customs official, resenting the man's presence. Beaumont held a clear contempt for the import processes this country enforced on him. But, like he had done many times before, he would grin and bear it.

Staring up at the towering metal which stood like a mountain in front of him, his mind could only focus on what was finally here. The smell of the stale sweat from the stevedores who milled around him would normally cause him to abandon such a locale as fast as he could - or if he had to stay, make his assistant Finney - who currently stood silently and obediently next to Beaumont - move them on forcefully or by bribe. He couldn't abide filth. But his mind couldn't even focus on that. Not here and now. Today was *too* important.

The customs official droned on mindlessly to Beaumont. He was too talkative even for a government agent. Far too talkative. Completely opposite to his assistant, Finney, who always knew only to speak when spoken to. Because of this, he often forgot that Finney was there and standing beside him. Beaumont felt that his assistant was indeed perfect for him, though more of a weasel than a man - in both looks and actions.

"I'm surprised you're here in person," the official said as he glanced down at the clipboard gripped in his hand. "The paperwork is completely in order. You could've just sent a driver, like everyone else does."

Rolling his eyes, Beaumont replied impatiently, "I've

waited a decade for this piece. I'm not about to let a prole of a delivery man lose it in transit."

Finney, noticing the custom official's expression showing some offense at the pejorative comment, cut in. "Mr. Beaumont negotiated personally with the Iranian government to obtain this piece. It's too important and valuable to leave anything to chance."

"Yes," the official replied, annoyed. "I do occasionally read the newspapers, you know. I'm not that much of a *prole*." He immediately disliked the assistant as much as he disliked Beaumont.

The mobile crane towering above the cargo ship suddenly burst to life as it spun left with a loud *WHIRRRR*. Large chains from the winch hung off its arm, swinging high above the dockside, and moving over the moored ship's deck.

Beaumont watched with studious intent.

The customs official glanced at his clipboard again, avoiding any more interaction with Finney, and spoke directly to Beaumont again. "Antiquarian sculpture. Eight foot tall. Of the pre-Islamic god... Uhhh..." The official tried his best to pronounce the words that followed. "Ah... Ahoora? Ahara?"

"I think you will find it is correctly pronounced Ahura-Mazda," Beaumont said.

"Mazda? Like the car?" the official asked.

Finney snickered at this plebeian observation. Beaumont grimaced, though his eyes remained on the ship.

He saw it, up on the winch. Strapped into large metal links, a crate was now lifted up by the crane. This was *his* crate. He could tell from the burned-in stamp which adorned its large wooden side. The Farsi text that had been branded into it stated it was *Property of Iran*. He found this amusing, as it was now anything but. He had enough money to buy any treasure from anyone. They all had a price; no matter the owner, be they a pauper or a ruler. He could afford whatever was demanded. For this particular piece, the claims of it being *'a holy relic of historical importance to the culture and history of Imperial Iran'* may have been true, but that did not matter. In Beaumont's experience, everything had a price. Especially history.

The official continued to read the forms on his clipboard. As his eyes scanned the text, he noticed the cost which had been listed for this item. He couldn't believe what he saw. That much money? For a lump of stone? He knew this man could afford it, but still... that much money for anything, no matter how old and rare, he just couldn't fathom.

"If you don't mind me asking, Mr. Beaumont, what makes this sculpture so... special? I mean, this thing cost more than the ship that brought it here."

His eyes still affixed to the crate, Beaumont spoke with a quiet reverence - more talking to himself than answering the official's redundant question. "This dates from the 12th century. Under Islam, praying to forbidden gods was persecuted and outlawed; Ahura-Mazda being one of these forbidden deities. A miracle that this piece was even made in that century. A bigger miracle that it survived in one piece."


Inside the crane, Mickey Carducci was not having the best of days. Last night had been another in a long line of him celebrating nothing in particular, sitting in a bar with no-one in particular. Because of this - when morning broke - he was yet again paying the price. He knew he wasn't a teenager anymore. He knew he couldn't tie one on without the punishment it wrought, and it had only been getting worse with every passing year.

Now deep into his 40s, it was only a matter of time before he drank so much that the pain would never go away. The precipice of alcoholism was probably behind him now; no matter, it would not stop him. He knew he was a hop, skip and a jump away from a slippery slope into his grave. He had accepted that. Who did he have to live for, anyway? The kids? They were taken when his wife left.

And, naturally, he planned to go out again tonight. *It'd be rude not to*, he thought to himself - one of the myriad of shallow aphorisms he repeated himself on a daily basis to justify his poor choices. He just had to stay awake and make it through the day. With a whiskey and Advil chaser gurgling inside him, in addition to the multiple coffees, the hangover ache which had struck his entire being was slowly subsiding. His bloodshot eyes, the exhausted expression, and the bleary feeling of cotton wool now taking up residence in his skull were the only bits of evidence that remind of the festivities of the previous night. Or so he assumed.

The sludge which tried to pass itself off as black coffee was his closest friend today. Now on his fourth cup of the shift, he waited for it to cool down. The steam billowed as it sat in its paper cup, precariously placed on the edge of the console in front of him. He would need *many* more before the shift ended.


"What the hell is he doing?" Beaumont said, his voice an anxious panic, as the crane swung the crate dangerously wide over the dock.

"Jesus!" Finney said, joining in, with an attempt at emulating his employer's shocked, angry tone. A real sycophantic yes-man through and through.

At the control station on the dock, the foreman shouted

angrily into his radio handset. "Hey Mickey, what the hell you doin'?"

Inside the crane, Mickey's hangover had reached stage two, suddenly hitting him with waves of nausea. Hearing his boss's message over the speaker in the cabin, Mickey tried his best to re-focus his attention on the job at hand. Seeing the crate swinging on the arm outside his window, he made a desperate grab for the levers in an attempt to steady the cargo.

As he reached forward, his inattentiveness caused his hand to clip the side of the paper cup. The coffee tipped over the edge and the molten liquid poured over the controls as well as Mickey's fingers, blistering him on contact.

"Fuck!" he said, through gritted teeth as his hand jerked back in pain, hitting the release lever. The winch voiced a loud, foreboding creak of a metal lock opening. Mickey's eyes widened in terror.

"No, no, no... *SHIT*!"

Beaumont, Finney, the government official, and all the stevedores stood on the docks gazing up in horror at the crane swinging.

Sensing something was wrong with the delivery, and like any good dog would do, Finney rushed toward the foreman, shouting. "What the hell does your man up there think he's playing at?!"

The foreman could see what Finney did not. The winch opening high above; the crate plummeting from the metal grip. Tumbling down at speed. Directly above Finney.

"*GET OUT OF THE WAY*!!" the foreman screamed. But, as

this last word was voiced, Finney, already glancing up, stood in a terrifying moment of realization, unable to move out of the way in the only second he had left. In that second, he knew that the oncoming shadow would be the certain cause of his demise.

Like a meteor striking the earth, the crate struck the asphalt with immense power. The sound, a cacophonous smash, echoed throughout the docks. The crate's wooden shell splintered in an instant, as the priceless statue inside shattered into a multitude of clay shards.

The surrounding men cowered as they hid from the flying debris. After a few moments, the noise faded, and everyone stared at the crashed remains.

"God no," Beaumont said under his breath, staring wide-eyed at the wood, metal and terracotta, which lay atop the decimated remains of his now-former assistant. The priceless sculpture, broken into many pieces of cracked clay, littered the ground around him. Whilst everyone else managed to move out of the way to avoid the flying debris, Beaumont had stood rigid, glued to the spot; unable to process any thoughts of self-preservation, much like Finney. He, though, remained unscathed by the accident. Instead of shock, or sorrow, Beaumont's face was an immovably affixed appalled expression. The disgust ran throughout his entire body. A disgust, though, not for his assistant's death - he didn't care about that at all. Assistants were a dime a dozen.

Priceless, one of a kind historical discoveries on the other hand...

With a snarl creeping over his face, Beaumont turned and shouted at the official. "You will pay for this, you will *all* pay for this!"

The official could only stare back at Beaumont. He could

not find a single word to say in reply. His mouth just hung agape, his eyes wide.

Without waiting a moment more, Beaumont grunted at the official in frustrated anger then stormed away.

The official, still in shock, turned back to the scene of the accident.

For all the workers on the dock, time had stood still. Frozen. An all-consuming silence blanketed the docks as every man and woman stared at the scene; wide-mouthed at the blood seeping from underneath the wood and clay debris. Beaumont's outburst hadn't even registered with them. Their focus was too fixed on the remains of Finney and the crate.

High up in the crane, still processing the chaos he had just caused, Mickey, too, could see the blood spilling out from under the remnants of the fallen cargo.

He wished he had a drink right now.

Soon the nearby dockworkers, as well as the official, swarmed over the scene, struggling to move the debris of the sculpture and crate off of the mangled corpse which had been crushed below it. Though they all knew that Finney had lost his life upon impact, they still rushed to clear the path above him out of pure instinct. As if, when cleared, the dead man would suddenly find renewed breath, and this nightmare of a day could be forgotten.

As workers moved the debris and the chunks of clay arms, feet, and body, a dockworker named Etchison reached down to pick up a piece of clay torso; a curved piece, with sharp edges. As he turned it over to find a better grip, he noticed something buried within its inside wall - something that glimmered in the light.

Looking around surreptitiously, he made sure that everyone else was focused on what they were clearing from the scene, and that no one was looking at him and what he'd found. Looking over his shoulder he now saw Beaumont had walked away - leaving others to clean up the mess, just as all wealthy people seemed to do.

Quickly and smoothly, Etchison bent down, making it look as if he was about to pick up the piece of statue lying beneath him, but instead, he grabbed hold of the *something* that protruded from the solid clay. Within seconds, he had it loose and hidden in his hand. Without anyone's eyes focusing on him, he moved to pocket the item. As he did, he managed to steal a quick glance at his prize. When he saw the fiery redness of the jewel, he smiled.

*Today was a good day*, he thought.

CHAPTER

# THREE

Deeper in the city, beyond Skid Row and its burgeoning streets filled with the destitute, the buildings steadily grew higher and higher with each passing block. The denim-clad majority of the lower-class denizens that were scraping by slowly morphed into finely clothed shoppers. In this high end part of town, the only dearth of wealth belonged to the smatterings of T-shirted gawking tourists, who visited this place, yet couldn't afford to purchase anything here. Amongst these high end store fronts, between a by-appointment-only jewelry store and a ladies fashion outlet (where the lowest priced item cost well into triple digits), sat Buried Treasure Auction House. Like a city branch of Sotheby's or Christie's, this building may have had a store-front facade yet was obviously only the public face of a larger and much more prestigious concern.

Walking through a pair of large glass double doors, Doug Clegg - in his mid-fifties, wearing a crumpled leather jacket - strode in. Not caring that he was far out of his element, he bore an air of confidence which few could ever break. Doug would look more at home if cast in a film as a gangster's heavy, instead of a high-class auction house on the moneyed side of town. With his slicked back receding hair, his obvious Italian descent, his large barrel chest, and air of no bullshit, he was almost a walking caricature.

Striding over to the reception desk, he smiled as he noticed an attractive girl in her early 20s, sitting behind the counter. Somewhat bohemian in appearance, she was dressed in a dark purple skirt with a loose-fitting white shirt. He could tell from her hair and makeup that when she was outside of this conservative environment, she would no doubt look significantly wilder. He liked that. He liked that a lot.

Reading her name badge, he spoke in a pleasant tone. "Hi, Shannon."

Somewhat taken aback by the lack of formality that normally permeated these interactions, her mouth hung open for a moment.

*How did he know my name?* she thought.

Noticing her surprise, Doug motioned with his finger to the name badge pinned on her shirt. "That's you, right? Shannon?"

With a smile and a breath of relief, she realized that this man wasn't, in fact, the most ballsy stalker in the world, she was just not very with it this morning. Adopting her most professional and friendly receptionist's manner she asked, "Can I help you, Sir?"

"Doug. Doug Clegg. No need for Sir. I ain't my pa."

"Of course, Mr. Clegg, how can I help?"

Rummaging around in his jacket pocket, he smirked. "This..." Pulling out a wad of wrapped tissue paper, he lay it on the counter in-between them. "I got a pawn shop down on union and Fifth. Y'know, that part of town that's the asshole of the armpit of the universe?" He unwrapped the tissue paper from the object within. "This arrived this mornin' and I kinda got a hunch about it, so bought it on the spot. Didn't even cheap shot him. Gave him a better price than I probably shoulda. So that brought me here. I think I need it appraised. Ain't your average shiny thing."

As the last piece of tissue came away, Shannon's eyes widened. She saw the opal that lay within, sparkling and shimmering from the light cast by the naked bulbs overhead.

"Beaut' ain't she?" Doug said with a certain amount of swagger.

Motioning to the gem nearer with her hand, Shannon asked "May I?"

"Sure, knock yourself out."

Picking it up, Shannon looked closer at its angled sides. The light seemed to reflect inside it forever. She was no expert in jewels by any stretch of the imagination, but she could tell that this was far too distinct to be simply a piece of mass-manufactured costume jewelry. "I think you made a smart move," she said under her breath, marveling at the crimson gem in her hand. *Then again,* she thought, *it could be glass, for all I know.*

"Nick?" she called across the room to Nick Merritt, a middle-aged man who had been busy checking the framing of a large painting that hung in the foyer. If ever a human could exude the air of being obsessive and greedy, it was Nick Merritt. Maybe it was the ostentatious yet pristine gold jewelry he wore too much of. Maybe it was the proprietorial glances he gave to all the treasures in this building, as he straightened and re-straightened every piece on display daily. One thing was for sure though, the expression *he would sell his own mother if the price was right* may well have been coined with him in mind.

Staring back to the reception counter, he replied in his whiny tone "Yes, Ms. Amberson? What is it?"

"We've got something I think my sister needs to look at," she replied, "can I borrow your expertise to make sure?"

Piquing his interest with her flattery, he walked briskly over to her. As he approached, he saw the opal sitting in her open palm, which she then held up toward him. He did a double take at the man who had brought it in.

*An obvious criminal*, he thought.

Taking the gem from Shannon's palm, he looked much closer at it as he held it up to the light.

"Quite fabulous," he said under his breath before turning toward Doug. "May I ask, what is the provenance?"

"Huh?" Doug replied, confused. He hated to feel stupid in front of anyone, but these types of people always confounded him with the ways in which they spoke to him. He better understood the toothless drunken degenerates who regularly stumbled into his store trying to sell stolen goods for crack money.

"In history," Nick clarified. "Where did it come from? Who owned it?"

"Oh, yeah. I bought it from a guy who said it's been in his family for years. Grandmother gave it to 'im. That's all I know. But it's mine now, whatever."

Nick shot Shannon a glance.

She knew him well enough that she could read his mind. It was the same look on his face that he made every time he said, *'If you believe that, I've got a bridge in Brooklyn you'll want to buy'.* She also knew that his need to keep this Italian man on the hook silenced any urge to say it aloud.

Turning back to Doug, Nick smiled a shark's smile; large and full of teeth. "I see. Alright. Tell you what. I'm going to take this to my very best appraiser. Shannon here will fill out a receipt for you. Is this amenable?"

Nick didn't even wait for an answer before he clasped his fingers over the gem, turned and walked away toward the rear of the showroom foyer, to where an electronically locked security door led to the offices and storage of the auction house.

Doug looked to Shannon with an unsure smile and said, "Guess I ain't got no choice, huh?"

Within one of the auction house's appraisal rooms, a desk littered with the tools of the trade - microscopes, reference books, swabs, lightboxes etc. - took up most of the room. Alex sat, partially hidden behind the appraisal gear. She was out of her gym clothes, dressed in business attire, and looking smart. Nick stood over her with an excited glint in his eye.

She was very tired. Nick had already run her ragged today, and it was only half past ten. At least it would be time for lunch soon.

Every item she was given to appraise was of "paramount urgency" and had to be done "immediately and without delay". It was no different this time. To make matters worse, he stood too close to her, expectantly. Watching as she held the opal to the bright light of her examination lamp. *Why won't he just let me work in peace?*

"So?" he asked impatiently, "is it as I hoped?"

"A fire opal this size is not cut by any faceter. It's..." Struggling for the correct words Alex could only say, "...wow. It's just, *wow*."

"Financially 'wow'?" he asked with a sudden grin, already imagining the possibilities of the income this stone might represent. Alex though, had barely heard his question. She twisted the opal against the light, entranced by its clarity.

"Excellent translucence." The words fell from her lips almost as though they were a mere train of thought. "No other color traces. It's... unique. Truly unique. I need to take a closer look."

"That is a good word. Unique. I like it when you use that. Should realize quite a price, yes?" He didn't need her to answer this. Her reaction had told him as much.

Still enchanted by the shimmer of the red stone, she replied, "Should get more than *quite* a price."

"I am honestly salivating, Alex! Get me a report as soon as possible. Okay? This is of paramount importance."

Alex nodded. For the first time she agreed. This item *was* that important. Nick smiled and exited silently. He was confident she would make this her top priority.

Laying the gem on the light box which was embedded into the top of the desk, she switched its lamp on. The light shone upward, illuminating the stone from beneath. Smiling, she realized that, for a change, she was actually *excited* to do her job. Maybe for the first time in years. The usual run of badly cared-for paintings, knock-off statues or tacky retro memorabilia was not what she had gone through all that doctorate training for. She wanted the rarest antiquities to study. She wanted the most obscure objet d'art there was. She wanted... the *unique*. Like this.

She could not wait to weigh it, measure it, examine every aspect of it with every single method at her disposal. But first, she grabbed the eye lens and pen light from the desk. She smiled as she looked closer. She swung the brilliant white beam from the torch over the jewel's surface, and stared at its insides, the lens firmly affixed to her focused eye.

Nothing could be this flawless and perfect, surely? There *had* to be flaws. Hadn't there?

"Wait a minute," she muttered, as her eyes focused on something deep within.

*What was that?*

As she moved the light slowly over the ruby-colored surface, she noticed a tiny black dot, deep, deep in its center. Imperceptible to the naked eye, but definitely there.

She sighed. "I guess nothing's perfect after all."

Removing the lens from her eye, she turned off the pen light, then moved the gem onto the microscope bed.

Adjusting the focus, she scanned the stone slowly, not only to get a clearer look at the flaw, but to see what other secrets it may be hiding. However, the detail at this magnification was refusing to come into focus with ease.

*There must be a fingerprint or something on it.*

Taking the gem from the microscope, she grabbed a nearby cloth and rubbed it onto the flat side she had looked through. Quickly holding the opal up to the examination light, she noticed some cloudiness on its surface. Bringing it up to her mouth, she breathed a deep lungful of air onto it and suddenly - at the edge of perception, like an echo from an unimaginable distance - she heard a sound like the sigh from a waking dragon; the sound of something great and awful rousing itself from a cursed slumber.

Startled, Alex glanced around the room.

*What the hell was that?*

But the room was empty. There was no one in here except for her. Listening for a few moments longer, she felt some relief as she shrugged off the uneasy feeling. It must have been her imagination, nothing more. A shiver ran down her spine.

*Someone walked over your grave again,* as her mom used to

tell her every time she felt a chill. She did not see the light within the gemstone glow for a brief second before it dissipated.

Cleaning the jewel on the cloth again, wiping the condensation from her breath away, she placed it again under the microscope and focused in for another look.

As she adjusted the aperture, she peered into the eyepiece. Her eyes quickly widened in shock. Whatever unseen residue she had cleaned off had exposed something deep within this jewel. Magnified 500 times by the lens of the scope, she stared at what looked like an organic tumultuous cloud, deep within its center. Like a cosmic nebula in miniature, heaving and turning over and into itself.

A hand touched her shoulder.

"*Jesus Christ*!" Alex shouted as she spun around in shock, startling Nick, who had come back into the room unnoticed.

He jerked his hand away, "Calm down, Alex! Christ!"

Crashing back to reality, she regained her composure with a sigh of relief. "You scared me, Nick! I didn't hear you come in." Nick looked unimpressed by her reaction. "I was... lost there for a moment."

"Wasn't five hours long enough to appraise a simple jewel?"

Stunned, Alex glanced up at the clock on her wall. Sure enough, 3:30 p.m.

*How is that possible?*

It was just before eleven last time she checked. As she pondered this conundrum, her stomach growled at her, radiating discomfort throughout her belly. She was starving.

"Come on, Alex," Nick said, "time is money. What's the verdict?"

Alex glanced uncertainly back to the microscope, then

checked the time on her watch, double checking the math. Where had the hours gone?

"Alex?"

"I think... there's something..." she said, uneasy, "...there's something wrong with it."

"Shit." That was the *last* thing Nick wanted to hear. "Does it affect its value at all?"

Alex shrugged weakly.

Picking up the opal from the microscope, she looked at Nick.

"I need to run some more tests," she said. "But not here. I need to use different equipment."

Her head started to throb with a familiar tension headache. She blinked hard, trying to shake it off.

"More tests..." Nick grumbled, as he turned to leave. "Typical."

CHAPTER

# FOUR

S t Marion's High School sat on the other side of the tracks, deep within the inner city. Though a large school, it solely catered to lower-income families of that district, meaning that it had the same issues as all inner-city schools. The buildings, though once proud when built, now stood mostly in disrepair. The fascia provided a convincing appearance that it was a well-cared-for and stringently maintained educational institution - but it was only that: A fascia. A pretense. A mask to cover the myriad issues within.

Alex strode purposefully across the campus quad. Her mind tumbled with the noise of uncertainty. This quad was packed with students. She guessed that classes must have just gotten out.

Alex looked at her watch. 5 p.m. *He would still be here.* She wished she knew where the time had gone today. Those three missing hours. Had she really just stared blankly at the gem for that long?

Slowing her pace, she came to a stop outside a large brick building. Despite having visited here many times before, all the campus's buildings looked the same. Which made them very easy to mix up. After seeing the sign 'Alina Hall - Department of Science', and confirming the location to herself, she smiled and quickly ascended the stairs.


Josh had been having one hell of a tough day. He had to put in a Herculean effort in order to keep focus. Teaching troubled kids who didn't care about science was difficult at the best of times. Teaching troubled kids who didn't care about science while your mind was distracted on matters of the heart was even worse. Each day had its struggles, but he couldn't stop thinking about Alex.

Sitting at his desk, he took a breath, stared at the mountains of unmarked papers in front of him, and sighed. The last class was done for the day. They all got to go home. He did not. He could relax only after he got through all these papers. *Then* he could go home. *Then* grab a bottle of wine and forget this place. *Then* also forget any heartbroken thoughts of Ale—

"Josh?"

Looking up, Josh saw Alex standing in the doorway of his classroom. *Of course*, he thought to himself. *Fate won't let me have a break for one night, oh no.*

Despite her sudden appearance tormenting his emotions, Josh was nonetheless happy to see her.


After Alex had finished explaining the reason for her visit and the mysterious gem that had come into her possession, Josh found himself surprised that she wanted his expertise, instead of his ear, as that was de rigueur. She only ever came to his work to see him when she was upset about something.

Not that he minded. But it was nice that, for once, she needed him for his mind, not his shoulder.

As he held the opal between his fingers, he noted to himself that it was surprisingly heavier than it first appeared. His interest piqued, he turned in his chair to Alex.

"Something inside it? Like what?" he said.

"I have no idea. But it's not a typical jewel flaw."

If Josh didn't know better, he would swear she seemed afraid of what she was talking about.

"Well, I guess I could give it a spectral analysis. See what readings it throws up. When d'ya need to know?"

Impatiently, Alex took a step closer to the desk. "Can you do it now?"

Josh motioned to the papers piled over his desk. "I gotta finish this for Herr Leiber first. Can you stick around for an hour or so? I can get to it then."

Pulling a frustrated expression, she shook her head. Though eager to know the mystery of this curious gem, she could not stay. "I can't. I gotta put my girls through their paces."

Josh nodded with a smile. "Ah, basketball night."

"Call me later? I really wanna know about this."

"The second I can, I promise."

Smiling, she leaned over the desk and gave him a hug. A platonic hug.

*For now*, Josh thought.

*For now*, Alex *also* thought.

"You're the best Josh," she said, planting a kiss on his cheek. "I owe you one, big time."

"Dinner and a movie?" *Christ Josh*, he thought to himself as the words escape his lips. *The first rejection wasn't enough?*

"How about hot dogs and a ball game?" She smiled, not

wanting to repeat the awkwardness of their conversation at the gym this morning.

Grinning, Josh turned back to the papers, picked up his red marking pen, and said, "You'll be sorry when I'm dead!"

Walking out, Alex said over her shoulder, "Only if you die before you do this for me."

"Oooof," he said, glancing up as she left. "Cold, Alex. That's pretty cold!"

Blowing him a kiss before finally disappearing from view, Alex felt better about their relationship than she had this morning. Not awkward at all. Just joking and fun - she hoped.

*For now.*

CHAPTER

# FIVE

Young legs ran, pounding on the hard wooden surface of the basketball court.

Weaving among the two teams of twelve-year-old girls, Alex ran with them. Keeping up, watching the action as it happened.

This wasn't a game, it was training - but Alex would make sure these girls played like a championship was on the line. They had to be ready. Ready to beat their next opponents. They were *her* little warriors. They would not be beaten. Well, that was the lie she told herself. They had not won a game in months.

One girl, Sierra, a waif of a child, and yet somehow the star of the team, leaped for the basket while she shot the ball. Sierra misjudged her aim, and the ball struck the side of the hoop, then rebounded off and flew back up the court.

Blowing the whistle around her neck, Alex quickly stopped the action. Beckoning with her hand, she motioned for the players to gather closer. "Sierra, that was real good. But..."

"But it was awful," said Sierra, out of breath and with a weary tone that belied her age.

"You know why you missed, right?"

The young girl shook her head and shrugged. "Didn't aim right, I guess?"

"Well there's that." Alex smiled before she continued, "But you took too much time finding the shot. You didn't have the *stillness* of place."

Like a hive mind with a singular thought of *What the hell is the coach talking about?* the girls simultaneously gave Alex confused faces.

"Look, all of you can put the ball through that hoop, as long as you refocus. *Know* the goal. Take a breath. Steady your aim." Though Alex was not the greatest player, she adored being able to impart cheesy wisdom to these girls. "Got me?"

A chorus of "yeah" and "sure" emerged from the team, though, they didn't really understand *exactly* what the coach meant.

Sensing that her message still hadn't landed, Alex further explained. "In a game, you don't have time to go at it at a snail's pace. Somebody's always gonna be trying to take that ball away from you. That's why you need the *stillness*."

The girls were no closer to understanding what this meant.

"Okay, you look a bit confused. Let me break it down. The stillness isn't in the body. It's up here." She pointed to her head. "If you get a chance at a shot, you have to forget *everything* else. Not the other players, they don't exist in this stillness. Time? To hell with it. Doesn't exist in this court. In that moment only two things exist. You and the basket."

"What about the ball?" asked one of the more precocious girls on the team.

Alex laughed. "Fine. *Three* things. At this moment. You, the basket and," she motioned back to the girl.

"The ball!" the girl said.

"Yes! So you are in this stillness, with the ball in your hand. No time. No other people. Just you three. So see it. Send it. You should know where it is at all times." As she finished, Alex saw that more was needed. "Okay, watch."

Picking the ball from the floor, Alex started dribbling it at speed as she walked backward to the basket, keeping eye contact with the girls while she moved.

"You need to see the goal in every second of the game. See it in your mind where the goal is at *all* times. And right now it's behind me about 20 feet away." She started to build up more speed, dribbling the ball faster. "So we know it's there. We just have to turn and find our aim. We don't stop, *then* see where the hoop is, which is what you did, Sierra. You should *always* see it in your mind. Record it. Don't erase it. Then when you are ready, if you know where the goal is at all times, you have the stillness to be able to focus, and—"

Now beneath the hoop, Alex spun, and without pausing, she jumped and released the ball. Rebounding off the backboard, it tumbled with purpose back down through the hoop. A perfect lay-up on display.

The girls burst into rousing applause, but as Alex's feet landed back down on the court, her whole body jolted, and she shut her eyes in agony.

As her body twisted, she opened her eyes. But she did not see the gym where she had been standing a second ago. Gone were the girls. Gone was the court. Gone was the whole gymnasium.

Instead, she saw a different, hellish and twisted reality.

A terrible laughter echoed through the chamber in which she now found herself. It seemed to fill the very air around her. She could hear the ominous searing whistle of an approaching and very violent storm. There were dark red walls in front of her. Something was moving - undulating - beneath those walls.

Trying to fathom what happened and where she was, all Alex could discern was the noise, the stench, and the darkness in the middle of this blood-red place. Suddenly, a darkness so brilliantly black it hurt her eyes to gaze upon it moved like the nebula had inside the stone.

A blistering wind gusted by. It carried a voice. A deep guttural malevolence which slicked every syllable that was uttered.

"You woke me..." it said with perverse glee.


"Ms. Amberson?" Sierra said in a panic as she stood over Alex. All the girls looked concerned, they stood in a semi-circle, staring wide-eyed down at her.

Alex suddenly opened her eyes. She looked at the girls, uncertain of her location.

"Sorry about that." She blinked a few times, then sat up unsteadily.

"Ms. Amberson? Sierra asked again. "You okay?"

Forcing a smile, Alex got to her feet, trying to maintain her balance as best she could. "Yeah. Yeah. I'm sorry. Got dizzy for a moment, that's all."

She noticed the ball from her shot was still rolling along the court; she must have only been unconscious for a second or two. Gems that made hours feel like seconds. And hallucinations that made seconds feel like hours. Could this day get any weirder?

Walking over to the ball, she picked it up, then without missing a beat, got right back into the lesson.

"Like I was saying. Stillness. It's where you focus your mind to be aware of what you need at all times, so you have more time for everything else you need to do to make that goal happen. Remember, this game is more about remaining still than being an ace shot!" She threw the ball to Sierra, who caught it without effort. "So, go on. Do as I did... just without the passing out. Okay?"

Sierra smiled, then the team spread out, giving her room to make another shot.

Alex clapped her hands and blew the whistle. As she put on a brave face and dove right back into the training session, she couldn't help but wonder *what the hell was going on?*


The sun had begun to leave the city, and within Alina Hall, the darkness fast approached.

Inside the laboratory, only one light remained switched on; A single lamp on the desk where Josh sat, worked busily. The shadows in the rest of the room grew darker and darker with each passing moment, as the final beams of the sun retreated.

Inside a miniature CAT scanner, the track which the Opal sat on was fed in and out of the scanner's central area. It was linked with long wires. Monitors and magnifiers were switched on, displaying images of the stone, both thermal and spectral. Diagnostic readings showed on the computer terminal as the lights scanned the gem.

Josh pressed a button to increase the speed of the track's movement, as well as the intensity of the light penetrating its translucent shell.

The phone on the desk next to him rang loudly, breaking his concentration for a moment. He ignored it and kept working.

*If it's important, they'll leave a message*, he thought.

After the fourth ring, the answering machine clicked on and played the outgoing message:

*"Hi. This is Josh Aickman, St Marion's High School... I'm probably turning lead into gold or finding a cure for cancer right now. So why don't you just go ahead and leave me a nice little message to brighten up my day."*

He smiled. Despite hearing the message nearly every day for the past three years, it still made him laugh.

Checking the gem's position on the monitors, he stared at the main magnification image of the stone's core.

In the scanner, four additional lasers jiggled into position around the opal and shone brightly. Beams of intense white light joined the others, all through the central core of the jewel. Josh continued to stare intently at the magnification monitor, looking away occasionally to the numerical results terminal - anxious to interpret the updated results with this increased resolution. With his focus intent, he did not notice the thermal imaging monitor. Nor, intent as he was on the readouts, did he see the heat pattern of the opal begin to swell and subside with the regularity of a newly beating heart. He was also too preoccupied to hear the tiny *hisssss* echoing in the room, as if originating from a great distance; a hiss laden with unholy excitement.

*"Josh? Hello? It's Me?"* Alex's voice called out from the answering machine. *"You there?"*

Looking over to the phone, Josh held his hand up, telling Alex to hold on, as if she were standing next to him.

"Shit. *One minute.* Gimme a minute," he called out. "Stay right there!"

He scoured the new data being shown on the monitors. He looked, in turn, at each screen. As he read the new numbers and saw the most recent visual scans, his jaw dropped.

"What the..."

On the answering machine, Alex continued, "*Maybe you're grabbing coffee or something. Listen, I'm going to keep talking 'cause you can't really call me back here. Well you could. But I wanna speak now dammit!*" She laughed.

Reaching for the switch, Josh killed the additional CAT Scan lasers, and looked back to the magnified image of the opal. He gasped as it moved in front of him.

The image showed the inside of the gem pulsing furiously as if a flame had burst to life within it. Turning off the additional lasers did nothing. The pulsing in the image only seemed to grow more intense. Yes, he was sure of it now, as the red glow clearly brightened and filled the room.

"*So, anyway,*" said Alex, "*how's it going? Find anything? Sorry to be impatient, but some really weird shit has happened to me today.*"

Hearing her words, all Josh could think was *Yeah? Well something weird is happening here too!*

Turning his attention from the monitors, to the opal in the machine, he noticed slivers of light appearing along its body. Two hairline cracks spread over its surface, like an egg on the precipice of hatching.

From somewhere not on this plane of existence, a low ominous rumble could be heard.

"Oh shit..." was all he could mutter. He guessed what was about to happen.

"*Where the hell are you?*" Alex continued with mock annoyance on the answering machine. "*C'mon pick up, pick up, pick up.*"

Josh made an attempt to run, but there was no time to escape. With a concussive roar reminiscent of an atom bomb, the entire CAT scanner exploded as the opal cracked apart into four large quadrants. It released hundreds of fire-red beams, each as narrow as needles, yet long as lances. Each as fast and deadly as guided missiles.

Without a moment to see what was coming, several beams shot into Josh's body, and ripped through the other side, as if he wasn't even there. He let out an agonized scream as the red-hot light seared into and out of his flesh. As they shot out, his innards broiled from the beams' extreme heat, his tormented wails lost among the deafening noise of exploding equipment, as the remaining beams tore through the many other pieces of scientific gear positioned around the lab.

Standing at one end of the now-empty basketball court, Alex looked at the pay-phone receiver in her hand. She moaned, annoyed. "You bailed on me? Dammit, Josh."

Suddenly staggering as if hit by a gigantic force, she gasped, her eyes opening wider and wider. As before, she was no longer seeing this court. Her sight was now elsewhere; a nightmarish vista once more.

The place had some familiarity. Though it was a hellish approximation, complete with red pulsing walls and a wailing wind - this was Josh's lab through an infernal eye.

Standing in the court, Alex's eyes streamed with tears. She was blind to the reality she actually stood in, only able to experience the vision thrust upon her.

In this distorted vision of Josh's lab, within the smoky ruins of desks and equipment, a figure - mostly obscured by smoke and debris - twitched on the floor. Groans of agony escaped from its lips. Sounds that were soon joined by another. The sound of something... slithering.

. . .

Then, as fast as it had come, the vision she was forced into disappeared in a blink of an eye. This episode, like the one before it, left her in a heartbeat, and she collapsed on the basketball court.

Blinking herself back to reality, she scrambled to her feet, reaching frantically for the phone receiver that now dangled from the wall. It was still connected to Josh's voicemail, recording her.

"Josh? *JOSH*!!" she screamed into the phone.


"Please, pick up."

But within Josh's lab, Alex's voice only bounced off the walls of the bombed out room.

The sprinklers had since burst to life and were now extinguishing small fires around the room as best they could. The smoke from the destruction crept over the rest of the debris littering the scene. A lot of the equipment had remained intact, but those hit by the opal's beams were left charred and destroyed beyond recognition.

Near a splintered worktable, the bent and burned remnants of the CAT scanner lay on a patch of scorched linoleum. The four fragments of the opal rested amongst the scanner's cracked and melted chassis, which glistened in the firelight.

In the midst of a large cloud of dust and smoke lay Josh's hideously wounded body. The lasers had burst through him like hot knives through butter. He gasped for air. He could feel that his organs had begun to shut down one by one, the heat of the lasers rendering them unable to continue their functions. He was only *barely* alive. His anguish at hearing

Alex's voice caused him to whimper and twitch. Unable to get to the phone. Unable to move at all.

*"Josh? Are you there?"* The panic in her voice grew more evident with each word spoken. *"Please pick up. Please. Oh God. Please. Please. Please."*

As Josh lay dying in his own misery, he thought he heard a noise; a scuffle across the other side of the room. It was probably nothing. He was here alone, after all. He knew he was. Yet he turned his head in the noise's direction anyway. He still grasped at the remote possibility that there was help here for him already. That he only had minor flesh wounds.

"Is someone there?" he said, his voice a pained gurgle.

A blanket of smoke covered the dark corner of the room where he had heard the noise originate. Hiding whatever was there.

"Hello?" he said.

Something within the smoke reacted to the sound of his voice. Something moved. Something twitched. Something that was small and shriveled. Something that glistened with blood like an aborted fetus from some alien's womb.

"Oh Christ..." Josh managed to wheeze through his collapsing lungs, as the *thing* crawled through the smoke toward him. It moved as if it was in as much pain as he was.

Closer.

Closer.

Josh tried to lift his ruined body from the floor, but he could not shift a fraction. He was dying quickly, and his whimpers of agony echoed loudly as he feared the inescapable eventuality the wounds had given him.

*"Josh... Please..."* Alex's scared voice echoed throughout the room.

With a *click*, the answering machine went dead; its tape

full. The only source of any possible comfort was stolen away when he needed it the most.

The creature moved up by Josh's head now. Its mottled flesh glinted with mucus, as though it had recently been skinned.

"Alex..." Josh whispered, closing his eyes. Praying for her to help him somehow.

The creature then spoke. In a pain-wracked whisper as weak as Josh's own voice, it echoed his sentiment. "*Aleeeex*"

Josh screamed in terror when he realized what lay beside him. The noise that came out of his lungs was an agonized ghost of his once-strong voice.

The creature spoke again, yet bizarrely there was now a hint of sympathy within the voice. "Iiis tthhhhe paaaaain terriblleeeee?" it hissed.

Staring wearily at the smoke-obscured horror, all Josh could do was nod weakly.

"I caan hellllp yooou," it said as it crawled closer. "I can eassssse your suffffferingggg."

Nearly silent, Josh replied, horrified. "This isn't happening. You're not real."

"Yes iiitt iisss! But iiit doessssn't haaave tooooo beeeee. I caaan stop iiiiit." It spoke in a hellishly serpentine voice, which, with each word, became deeper and deeper. Stronger and stronger. "Alllll yooooou haaaave to doooo issss ask."

The searing pain jolted through Josh as his body tried its best to stave off the freight train of death headed for him.

"Oorr I caan leave you on your owwwn." The creature cackled lightly as it spoke, as if it were enjoying this. "Iffff thaaat is what yooou want?"

"I," Josh began. Blood then pooled in his throat, as he choked "I want it to stop."

There was a pause, where all that could be heard was the

crackling of the remaining fires and smatterings of sprinkler water hitting the floor.

Then the creature spoke. Its voice low, assured.

"As you wiiish..."

For a moment, nothing happened.

Then, Josh screamed; screamed as hundreds of jets of blood suddenly burst from every one of the wounds which covered his body. Spewing out, as if from pressurized hoses.

Beneath him, his blood pooled outward like a nightmare snow angel.

Something else happened too; the creature shuddered with new life. Rippling with energy, it drew strength from this granted wish. As it shook, it grew in size with each second that passed. And with each change, the slithering creature proceeded to take on slightly more humanoid form.

Within seconds, Josh had no blood left in his body; his skin was a white, wrinkled covering on a sunken shell, still trembling from immense shock. As he died, he had only one thought - one silent sentence of four words: *I love you, Alex.*

The creature, still weak and partially deformed, though considerably stronger than before, stumbled to its feet. Its claw-like hands, resembling something three evolutionary stages away from completeness, stretched out.

From within the remains of the CAT scanner, the four quadrants of the opal flew out and landed in the creature's clawed palm.

A sigh of bestial satisfaction escaped its mouth as it disappeared into the smoke and headed out of the laboratory.

# Witness to the Infernal

CHAPTER

# SIX

As she sprinted across the grass of the campus quad, Alex felt the already apocalyptic panic explode within her when she noticed the police cars and the ambulance that were parked, lights flashing, outside Alina Hall.

"Oh my God," she said, her breathing erratic. She slowed to a stop, watching as a stretcher was carried up the steps and into the building. "No..." she said weakly.

Amidst the chaos of an investigative team - uniformed police officers, a plain-clothed detective, crime scene photographers, EMT's, the coroner - Alex stood at the entrance to the destroyed laboratory, stunned and appalled at the devastation in front of her.

The team of police workers were all too busy to notice her, all except for Detective Nathanson, who quickly rushed over.

"Ma'am, you are not supposed to be here," he said, standing between her and the mutilated body lying on the floor at the other side of the room. Looking past Alex, over her shoulder, he addressed a uniformed policeman who stood stoically by the door. "Isn't it *someone's* job to stop people just walking into here?" He gave the man no chance to reply. "It's yours, right? Shouldn't you be outside securing the scene?"

The policeman stared back at him with some contempt. Nathanson was young and scrawny, and looked every bit his age. The policeman, easily twenty years Nathanson's senior wasn't happy with being talked to like that. What did this kid know, anyway?

"So?" The detective continued, "Go do your job and stop anyone else contaminating the scene!"

With an annoyed sigh, the policeman walked out without a single word uttered. The kid wasn't worth his pension, he mused. But he liked to think that if he wasn't relying on it, he would've socked that arrogant prick square in the face months ago.

The detective then turned his attention back to Alex. "Please, ma'am. You cannot be in here."

Alex paid no attention to him, instead she stared toward the other end of the room. Transfixed by the body on the floor, dressed in what she could tell had been a white lab coat, but was now a scorched shred of charred fabric.

Her stomach sank in distress. "Please, God no," she said as tears broke down her face. "Josh..."

Nathanson silently cursed himself for not blocking the scene well enough from her.

Taking her arm, partly to comfort her, partly to stop her getting any closer to the body, Nathanson guided her a few steps back.

Gasping, Alex's tears multiplied into torrents as she got more and more hysterical.

"Easy, easy." Nathanson spoke calmly.

Turning pleadingly to the Detective, Alex stared into his eyes.

"Please. Please tell me that's not Josh. It's not him. He can't be..." She couldn't say it. It was all too much to fathom.

"I'm sorry," Nathanson said, trying as best as he could to keep his tone of voice even and soft, just as he'd been trained. Last thing he needed was a scene contaminated by someone grieving. This was his scene. He knew no one respected him as a detective at his age, but that was not his concern. He just wanted to follow the rules as best he could. He wouldn't lower himself to the pettiness he knew that others felt towards him. But if he didn't get her out of here, he would never hear the end of it. He had seen other more seasoned detectives suffer ridicule because of lesser mistakes.

"My name is Detective Nathanson, I'm the lead investigator here. You are, miss?"

As her gaze started to drift back toward the body on the floor, Nathanson repeated, "Miss?"

Steeling herself, she scrambled to straighten her mind from the feeling of being on an out of control rollercoaster. Falling further and faster downward.

"Amberson. Alexandra Amberson. Alex."

"And I take it you knew—" He was going to say 'the deceased', but managed to catch himself in time to spare her that particular phrase. "—Josh?"

"We're friends. Old friends. Best friends." She closed her eyes as more tears slicked down her cheeks. "I loved him," she managed to say before breaking down into sobs. Losing him was not something she'd ever thought could happen. They had their lives ahead of them to be together. To one day *really* be together. When she could get over herself and pull her shit together. Now though, all those dreams had died.

Nathanson, a little awkwardly, put his arm around her shoulder, allowing her time to cry. A comfort to her in her time of despair, giving her the moment to pull herself from this wave of grief.

Wiping her eyes, she stepped away from Nathanson. She couldn't do this in public. It helped no one.

"You wanna sit down?" Nathanson asked, motioning out of the door, aware he still needed her to leave the scene.

"No. No. I'm sorry." She sniffed as she forced herself to appear calm. "I'll be okay. Just please, tell me. What happened to him?"

"It's an ongoing investigation, but I can tell you that I don't suspect any foul play." Truth be told, he always suspected foul play. That was the default setting of any detective worth their salt. This was just more *probable* to have not involved foul play. "In all likelihood it was an accident. Equipment malfunction at a preliminary guess."

Alex's gaze traced over the scene, over the debris littering the room. The scorch marks on the linoleum. As she glanced about the room, Nathanson looked at her. He might be young, but he had earned his job through hard work and a keen eye. He could see that she was not just looking *at* things, but looking *for* something.

"You got any idea what it was he was working on?" Nathanson asked as casually as he could manage.

Alex regarded him, pondering whether she should lie to him or not. She immediately dismissed this question. What possible reason did she have to lie?

"He was analyzing a gemstone," she said, trying to block out the view of the coroner at work inspecting Josh's body, in the corner of her vision. "A fire opal. He was doing it because I asked him to."

Nathanson noticed the look of concern that fell over her face, as she tried to reconcile the link between Josh's death and his favor to her.

"I'm sure some jewelry couldn't have had anything to do with this accident." Nathanson motioned to the door with his hand. "Now please. Can we go outside? You really should not be in here."

# CHAPTER
# SEVEN

Not too far from the glow of the police lights over the campus grounds, the streets in this area soon became home to the desolate. A place where each alleyway and sideroad became part of an urban maze of hostility and desperation. A place permeated with violence, alcoholism, narcotics, and infected sexual encounters.

The few businesses that occupied this side of town were all prepared for any potential criminality that may come their way. Each had barred windows and security systems. Those storefronts without glass - due to vandalism - had boarded up windows, complete with their own crudely scrawled messages on them assuring people that they were still open. Each storekeeper who plied their trade here had no choice but to keep a trusty firearm at hand just in case that one bad element chose to single them out. This occurrence happened frequently.

At this time of night though, on this particular street, only one store remained open - a pharmacy. A nurse turned to walk inside on her way home from a late shift at the local hospital, but was quickly stopped by a homeless man slouched on the sidewalk just to the side of the entrance's sliding doors.

"Spare some change for an old altar boy, missy?" he slurred with a grin.

Avoiding him, the woman rushed inside without even making eye contact.

Calling tonight a lost battle, with none of the store patrons even sparing a dime for him, the homeless man stood up clumsily and looked around. Inside the store, he saw the nurse speaking to the pharmacist, who then turned and looked out to the entrance, angrily. Gesturing for the nurse to stay where she was, the pharmacist walked to the door, opened it, and looked sternly at the homeless man standing outside.

"How many times I gotta tell ya?" the Pharmacist yelled. "Quit bothering the customers!"

The homeless man smirked and said, "Hey, you left customers unattended in there. That's no way to run a business!"

Biting his lip, the pharmacist had had enough, and lost any remaining cordiality. "Don't tell me how to run my business, you fuckin' bum!"

"Then don't you come out here and tell me how to run my life, you sanctimonious prick. I can talk to anyone I want. You know where we are?"

"*My* store," the pharmacist retorted.

"No! this is the United Goddamn States of Goddamn 'Merica!" The homeless man started to raise his drunken voice as he pointed toward the ground. "This goddamn sidewalk belongs to the city. The city belongs to the state. The state belongs to the United Goddamn States of Goddamn 'Merica!"

The Pharmacist glared at this filthy, drunken man. "You know what? This *is* my sidewalk, and you know why?"

The homeless man stared back, wide-eyed, just wanting to punch him.

"'Cos I pay my fucking taxes, that's why. Now get the hell away from here before I call the cops on you again."

Swiping the air at the pharmacist in annoyance, the homeless man stumbled backward and grumbled, "Fuck you... I got somewhere I need to be, anyways."

Before disappearing back inside, the pharmacist flipped the homeless man his middle finger and grinned triumphantly.

Staggering off, the homeless man grumbled incoherent threats. Crossing the road, his anger built up until he stopped and called back to the store, "I hope you die you sack of shit! I hope you die and crawl past me in the gutter so I can piss on ya!"

The pharmacist was long gone; back at the counter serving a customer.

As the homeless man walked further down this increasingly desolate street, he staggered by another store doorway, albeit a closed one. Deep in the shadows, something moved, catching his eye. He might be drunk. He might be addled from years of drug abuse, but he definitely saw something from the corner of his eye. He stopped dead in his tracks. This was one of *his* doorways. This whole street was his. Everyone knew that.

Turning and looking in, he tried to focus on the moving shadow inside. "Hey! Who's there?" Taking a step nearer he continued, "This is my spot, you know that, right?"

"I ammm a frieeennd," the low voice rasped from the concealing darkness.

The homeless man looked confused.

"Did you reaaaally mean those curses yoooou hurled so freeeeely at that maaaan?"

Forgetting that this dark stranger was on his turf, the homeless man couldn't help but reply to the unusual question. "Damn straight, I meant it. That prick's a fucking prick."

Taking a battered pack from his pocket, the homeless man drew out one of his precious few cigarettes. One that wasn't a secondhand discard, like his usual brand. This was a luxury for most people in his situation. Lighting it, he took a drag and stared into the darkness of the doorway. "You new round here?"

"What would you giiiive to have those curses come truuuue?" said the voice.

"What?" The homeless man's focus swayed. "What you say'?"

"What would you giiiive," the voice repeated, and paused for effect, "to have those curses come truuuue? What would you giiiive to the being who could manifest thaaaat punishhhhment?"

Smiling, the homeless man let out a cracked laugh. "Ha! If a cigarette and a handshake ain't payment enough, then you're shit out of luck, pal. 'Cos that's all I got!"

"Not quite truuuue." The shadowed figure seemed to get closer while still remaining shrouded. "You have a soul you could bargain with."

Laughing hollowly, the homeless man took another drag on his cigarette. "Yeah right. I'd cash that thing for a shower and a bottle of Jack if I could."

"Really?" the voice said. "Then the death of your enemy would be considered a bargain, for this morsel?"

Grinning and nodding, the homeless man smiled. Sure, this guy, whoever he was, was encroaching on his place, but at least he was entertaining. He might even let him stay there the night. "You're one fucked up guy, I'll give you that. But you know what? I like the way you think." The homeless man's face then spread into a grin as a cruel joke formed in his mind. "But he should only get cancer. He should only get cancer and die."

Laughing, the homeless man took another drag on his cigarette.

And the voice from the doorway said, "As you wish."


While the nurse paid for her things, the pharmacist looked up and around the store, at the three other customers milling around. He then glanced up at the corner mirrors. He couldn't neglect these, or else some assholes could come in, hide from view, and try to rob this place.

*Not tonight. Not ever,* he thought. Under the counter, he had his Remington ready to go at any given moment, and he would not hesitate to use it at the first sign of trouble.

"You know what I say?" he said to the nurse before she turned toward the exit, "Government should round them bums up, and put 'em all into camps. Scum of the earth. Welfare checks and food stamps. Bleeding this country dry."

The nurse smiled politely, unsure of why this man would say something so hateful. They didn't know each other, and she wished she hadn't mentioned the homeless guy outside. The whole incident had been so unpleasant, she had hoped to put it out of her mind. But the pharmacist continued.

"And another thing. These S.O.B.s use this place like their own personal begging ground. I think they all—"

The pharmacist stopped short, surprise washing over his face.

Surprise that suddenly turned to agony. He slowly

staggered backward, leaning on the wall at his back for support.

"Are you okay?" the nurse asked.

Screaming as molten pain shot through every one of his nerve-endings at once, the pharmacist pushed himself forward, staggered around the counter-top, and onto the store floor, moving as if trying uselessly to outrun an invisible threat. The strength drained from his body at speed as he fell helplessly to the carpet, his screams calling the attention of the other customers, who walked over to see what was going on.

He could hear them speaking to him, shouting questions, as well as asking each other things, but he couldn't discern a single word over the noise of his own screams.

Glancing up, he could see someone standing outside, looking in at him. It was the homeless man. Watching. Aghast. Mortified.

The customers milled around the pharmacist in a panic. The nurse rushed over to the counter, picked up the telephone and quickly dialed 911. She knew whatever was happening to him was beyond her training as a maternity nurse.

Over the pharmacist's body, large dark brown patches appeared, his pale flesh being eaten up under the changing hue. Deadly untreatable melanomas which would have normally taken months to appear on someone, grew and spread in mere seconds.

He gazed at the nurse who had kneeled down beside him. "Help me," he said, weakly. "Dear God, help me..."

The nurse could hear his voice as it strangled itself, the melanomas growing inside his throat now, too.

"Somebody, do something!" one of the other customers shouted in a panic.

"What's happening to him?" said another, "Can we do anything?"

"Call for an ambulance, *now!*" the nurse replied with urgency. Looking back down to the man she then noticed that the melanomas not only covered every part of his visible skin, but were also, impossibly, on his eyeballs. Some of them bubbled out, becoming furious-looking growths. Ones which burst grotesquely as quickly as they'd grown.

As the slime and pus oozed out from the near-putrescent, choking body in front of them, the customers could only stand and stare - their emotions held in check by the impossible horror which they witnessed.

Finally, mercifully, the pharmacist shuddered, and then collapsed, dead; his body a pale, fleshless thing that looked like tortured skin which had been pulled loosely around some distorted skeleton.

Meanwhile, outside, the homeless man looked in at the scene, his mind unable to process what had happened.


A few streets away, in Alina Hall, Alex had collapsed in the corridor outside of Josh's laboratory. Although she didn't know it, she was looking through the eyes of the homeless man. And what she saw horrified her. Detective Nathanson held her arm to steady her. She couldn't understand this. She again was a witness to a hellish other world. Her hands twitched at her face as she couldn't quite believe the sight she had witnessed. Gasping in shock and distress, Josh's lab was somewhere very far away. She couldn't hear anything Nathanson had said to her.

All she could focus on was the death of a pharmacist that somehow played out before her eyes. But - as she was simultaneously inside the lab as well as the pharmacy - the blending together of the two locations was a twisted, unreal vision. A place skewed by a terrible unreality. The wind carried with it, a stench of death. She witnessed an other-worldly version of the cancerous fate of the pharmacist.

Grabbing a nearby chair, Nathanson lifted Alex up by her arms, then sat her down.

"Are you alright, ma'am?"

As the pharmacist's life ebbed away, Alex's vision slowly returned to the reality she had been in only moments earlier. A red mist dissipated from her eyes, and as the oppressive soundscapes died out in her ears, the corridor came back into view.

"Ma'am?" Nathanson repeated, louder. Trying to get through.

Regaining some semblance of composure after her vision, Alex looked up at the Detective. Blinking rapidly, she replied, "I... I don't know."

In the pharmacy, the customers all stared at the now-deceased pharmacist, not knowing what to do. No words spoken. Just frozen to the spot. Instead of considering whether they should wait for the ambulance to arrive, or to go home - they remained in frozen silence.

Outside, the homeless man backed away from the window; his alcohol buzz from earlier now totally vanquished. Sobriety was back with a bang, forced into him by what he saw in the pharmacy window.

"Jesus... Fucking.... Christ!" he said, as he took the stub of the cigarette from his lips. Then he dropped it to the ground, as if that itself had been the instrument of the pharmacist's destruction. He slowly fell to his knees, trying to make sense of what he had just seen.

Behind him, in the closed store's doorway, a figure emerged from the shadows. Within moments, a long shadow fell over the dropped cigarette. A shadow which caused the homeless man to look up to see what had cast it.

What the homeless man saw was the face of the creature who had granted his wish. But somehow, this creature had become altered. When it had first revealed itself, it was in a horrific state, with borderline incomplete features. A distortion of a man. Now though, it looked less uncanny and mostly whole. Though still misshapen in parts and covered in slightly scaly skin, it appeared fundamentally more human than it had only five minutes earlier.

Wrapped heavily in ragged clothes stolen from various dumpsters, the figure also wore a hat, which mercifully hid its monstrous visage from any clear view.

"Was it worth it?" the figure asked.

The homeless man would have sworn he had heard whispers in the wind. Looking around, he realized that the darkness now seemed to have gotten thicker - the shadows longer - as if their very existence had been attached to this figure, and it had brought the darkness with him. The wind seemed to have picked up too. And on the wind, a stench of rot.

Now looking up at the creature, the homeless man recognized an evil he hadn't noticed before. Backing away in terror, he scrambled to his feet and soon broke into a run down the street.

With a smirk, the creature bent over and picked up the discarded, still smoldering cigarette. Lifting it closer, it inspected the cigarette as if it had never seen one before. Putting it to its lips, it mimicked the homeless man and took a tentative drag. As the figure exhaled, it shouted after him, "Run insect. Run and tell *who* you will, *what* you will. Tell them. Tell them *all* something is loose in this city of corruption. Tell them there is something feeding on wishes. Tell them I shall raze the buildings of bricks to dust."

With a smile, it took another long and deep drag of the cigarette. With a satisfied grin it shouted after him again, "But tell them fast. Before I collect what is owed."

CHAPTER

# EIGHT

Inside their apartment, far away from Skid Row and far away from Josh's lab, Alex and Shannon sat. Alex was crossed-legged on her sofa and stared out of the window at the view of the city. Dressed for bed in a baggy T-shirt and shorts, she smoked a cigarette. Though no longer a habitual smoker, she had the very occasional need of a nicotine fix. Something to calm her nerves. Something to stop her from tearing her hair out in anguish. But tonight, it seemed more mechanical than medicinal. The taste of each puff sat sour in her mouth.

The day had taken its toll on her. First, the missing hours in the appraisal room, then the strange visions she had been experiencing, and finally Josh's horrific death. The grief gnawed at her insides like an emotional parasite.

On the opposite sofa, Shannon was also dressed in her pajamas. Her presence was something that Alex was so glad to have, even if they were not always on the same page. She felt more complete with her sister nearby. When buying this apartment, Alex had felt that the vacant second bedroom made the place feel more temporary, less complete. So, last year, when Shannon had accepted her invitation to move in, the apartment had finally felt like a home.

Shannon motioned to her sister's cigarette. "You're not enjoying that, are you? Look at your face."

Alex shook her head and took another drag

"Then put it out," Shannon scoffed.

Exhaling, Alex sighed. "They used to help me."

"Two years since you quit," Shannon replied as she watched her sister take *yet another* drag and pull a nauseated expression.

Finally relenting, Alex took the cigarette from her mouth and stubbed it out in an ashtray.

"I'll tell you what's gonna help you," Shannon said. "Doctor Montiglio's pills."

"Montiglio?" Alex said, surprised. "Jeez, it's been *five years* since I quit them."

"Then what are they doing in your medicine cabinet?"

"I keep the prescription filled."

Shannon looked confused.

"Safety net," Alex said. "Placebo. If I know they're there. I won't need 'em."

Shannon laughed, "Like *that* logic works. Just take a fucking pill, Alex."

"I don't need a fucking pill!" Alex glanced at the half-pack of cigarettes resting on the table. Briefly, and out of some masochistic ritual, she considered lighting another that she did not want or need. "I'm really okay. I'm just upset, Shan."

Shannon leaned forward, her expression caring. "Babe, you're not just upset. You know that, right?" Alex looked up from the pack to her sister, about to refute her claim. But Shannon continued, "You're seeing things! You said as much. Just like last time. I'm really worried."

Shannon knew that Alex was not being entirely truthful.

That was the only time she referred to her as *Shan*. When she tried to lie to her, for some reason she always used that abbreviation. Nobody called her Shan. Except Alex, who was saying it a lot.

"Don't worry, Shan. It's not as bad as last time. Please, drop it." Alex wanted this conversation over. "Go to sleep. All is okay, totally okay."

"Oh, for Christ's sake, Alex. Can the big sister act for just one night - *listen* to me."

Alex tried not to shout her reply.

"It's not an act. I *am* your big sister, Shan. I'm responsible for you!"

"Responsible?" Shannon's eyes went wide. "You brought me out to LA, gave me a place to stay. Doesn't mean you control me. You have to hear what I'm saying."

Alex closed her eyes, her head aching with tension. She consciously forced herself to appear more relaxed. She couldn't lose control. This couldn't become a *thing*. She and Shannon regularly shouted at each other just like any siblings did. But today was not a day she could handle that. Not on top of... of Josh.

"I really don't need this now," she said. "Can we talk about it another day?

Remembering her sister's loss, Shannon softened. "I'm sorry." She hated seeing Alex going through this. "And I'm *really* sorry about Josh. But you have to know it's not your fault."

With tired and heavy eyes, Alex looked back out the window. Her voice was quiet and worried.

"I can't see how this isn't all 'cause of me."

"What?"

Shannon couldn't quite believe what she was hearing. How could Alex think this?

"Before you say I'm all innocent," Alex said, "If I didn't give him that fucking stone-"

"It was just a jewel!" Shannon said. "And I was the one that gave it to you in the first place, so by that logic I'm to blame too. I could have just told that pawnbroker to fuck off. But I didn't, and it's not our fault. It's an accident. Babe—"

"If it was just a stone, I'd maybe agree."

Shannon sighed.

"Right. The weird thing that you saw. What do you *really* think a flaw in a chunk of priceless rock could do?"

"I think that's what killed him," Alex said.

"Do you have any idea how crazy that sounds?"

"Yeah. That's the problem. I know *exactly* how crazy it sounds. But I'm not crazy. I just... gotta process it all."

Within a twisted perspective across a murky vista, the air hung thicker than usual, the streets snaked around multitudes of dark houses, intertwining with each other in an eternal loop; an inescapable asphalt maze. The houses looked as if they had been carved from obsidian by some lunatic expressionist. The grass and trees all pulsed with a red glow and had the texture of stripped flesh. This was a version of a suburban landscape, as if designed by a demonic architect.

The sky was as black as pitch. The moon sat low, dulled and unable to illuminate much of anything. It hung like a pattern in the heavens more than a solar reflecting celestial body.

In front of a house, or more precisely a solid black representation of one, Alex now stood, still dressed in her nightclothes; ripped from *her* world, and standing in *this* one. She stared at the crooked path before her. Somehow, she knew she had to cross it. Hesitantly, she stepped onto the concrete. Slow step by slow step, she walked toward the front door. She knew this house. This was the family home. The one where the fire stole her parents away. The fire which she saved Shannon from.

When only halfway across the path, she jerked in shock as flames suddenly erupted from out of the house's carved windows. The flames billowed higher and higher - wilder by the moment.

Blood-curdling cries sprang from inside the inferno. Panicked, Alex ran up the porch steps and beat frantically on the black stone front door. She was reliving *that night* all over again through a nightmare lens.

No one answered. Inside, the screams and fire raged on.

With one hand, she thrust her hand into her shorts pocket - innately knowing the keys to the house were there. She pulled out a ring of three identical black keys. Without having any time to question, she scrambled to find the needed key to the door. But as she moved each key toward the lock, their consistency started to shift. Each one she held, in turn, bent out of shape as if suddenly constructed from a kind of jelly.

"Please, please, please," she said to herself and she tried to thrust the soft keys into the door lock. Becoming more hysterical, Alex looked up and screamed at the door, "Mom, Dad, Shannon!" she called.

Another explosion inside, as flames burst out of the hollow window frames.

*Nooooooo!*"

Jerking in shock, Alex woke up from the nightmare. Blinking, she tried to regain her focus. The light from the room almost blinded her.

"Alex? You really fall asleep? Am I that easy to beat? I can't even keep you awake?"

Looking up in a daze, the glare subsided and Alex recognized that she was in the racquetball court with Josh. She was sitting on the same bench in the same court where she'd played earlier that morning.

And there he was.

Alive.

Looking at her with his wonderful smile.

He pointed down to her feet.

Her head clearing, she glanced down to where he motioned, and noticed that the ball was sitting at her feet. With a smile of her own, she bent down and picked it up. Then she straightened and looked up at Josh again.

But he was gone.

No longer in front of her.

Turning to her side, the wind was knocked from her lungs. She saw that Josh now sat beside her. But this was not the *same* Josh. Instead this was a rotten, putrefied and repulsive version of Josh. The living corpse of her friend, who now looked at her with his empty, festering eye sockets. He moved his retracted lips and showed off his decayed teeth in a sickening grin.

He spoke with a distorted, low, thunderous voice; a cruelty in his timbre that hit her ears like a straight razor cutting her jugular.

"Ready to play, Alex?"


Screaming, Alex scrambled in her bed, sat bolt upright and struggled to catch her breath. The sweat slicked off her, looking as if she had just stepped out of the shower and neglected to dry herself.

In the darkness of her bedroom, she felt some relief and glanced at her bedside clock. It read 3:00 a.m.

The bedroom lights suddenly switched on. Shannon rushed in with a look of worry. No longer dressed in her pajamas, she now looked as though ready for a night on the town. She had obviously not gone to bed after their talk.

"Alex, are you okay?" Shannon sat down on the bed next to her.

Still coming out from her nightmares, with a grogginess she had trouble shaking, Alex simply nodded with a weak smile.

"Please. Can you just take one?" Shannon asked, reaching for a small bottle of pills. "I know you don't wanna, but please. For me. Just humor me."

Taking the bottle from her, Alex looked at the label and shook her head.

"I can't. These won't do any good." She dropped the bottle onto the bed.

"For fuck's sake." The exasperation exploded from her younger sister. "It's what they're for!"

Grabbing the bottle from the bed, she slammed it down onto the bedside table with a grunt of disgust. She stood up from the bed. She was over this, and ready to leave. She wanted to be here for her sister. But this was fast becoming the Alex show. She was becoming the martyr who would accept no help.

"Wait," Alex said as she noticed her sister's clothing. "What are you wearing that for?"

"I went out," she said, shrugging. "*Massive White Bias* at the Whiskey. Caught their last few songs. You crashed out. Didn't think you'd mind."

"Christ, Shannon, it was midnight when I went to bed!"

"So the fuck what?" Shannon said. "As I told you earlier, you don't control me. I went to meet some friends."

"You took the car?" Alex said.

"Yes, I took the damn car." She'd had enough of trying to justify her life to her older sister. "Sorry I didn't put that request in writing to you. Anyway, this is about you, not me."

Shaking her head, Alex ran her hand over her face.

"What about work? You can't just go out and—"

"Jesus!" Shannon cut her off, having enough of Alex's self-denial and incriminations. "It's fucking Pavlovian with you. Get your own shit together and stop worrying about me. The fucking fire was six years ago. You got me out, okay? I'm suitably grateful. But I'm not a child anymore. Just leave your judgement the fuck away from me. *You* are the one in need here, and I'm trying my fucking best to be there for you."

"Why did you bring that up?"

The events from Alex's nightmare were far, far behind her. Now she was just faced with this hardship. And her exhausted mind didn't have the energy for it right now. "Do you blame me cause I didn't get Mom or Dad out?"

"*Couldn't*, not didn't! *Couldn't! Couldn't!* Not your fault! Just like Josh is far from being your fault." She motioned to the pill bottle. "So stop blaming yourself, or that whole fucking thing is gonna start again!"

Glancing at the bottle, then back to Shannon, she reconsidered her motivations.

*No,* she thought. This was not a breakdown. This was something... else.

"This is different, Shannon." She could not give in. "Something's going on. Something *bad.* I know you don't understand, but I have to find out what it is, with a clear head. Not one clouded by those pills."

CHAPTER

# NINE

With the debris now long cleared, and the bloodstains scrubbed off the stone, the dockside carried on as if nothing bad had ever happened here. It was just another day and another ship that carried a whole new roster of items to unload. Alex stood at the dockside, sticking out like a sore thumb, as she questioned a worker.

"Etchison," the stevedore said, as he untied the knotted rope he twisted in his hands. "That's him over there." Nodding with his head, the stevedore motioned to a nearby worker who moved small boxes onto a forklift.

Nodding to the worker in thanks, Alex walked over to where Etchison was focused on his stacking, totally oblivious to the woman now walking his way. The other dockers were not as distracted by their employment. They all glanced her way appreciatively as she walked by them.

"Mr. Etchison?"

After placing a box onto the fork-lift, Etchison turned to this approaching stranger. Looking her up and down arrogantly, he whistled.

"Sweetheart, you can call me anything you like."

Alex's smile didn't falter as she replied with determination, "I'm not here to play games."

Letting out a laugh and appreciating her moxie, Etchison replied, "Well, that's one hell of a damn shame. Coulda been fun." He grinned flirtatiously, at least he thought it was flirtatious. Alex, however, thought it looked disgustingly predatory.

"Save it for the strippers, pal. I wanna talk to you about the opal."

Taken aback, the smile fell from his face.

"The jewel?" Alex said.

Etchison's manner changed on a dime. Gone was any welcoming flirtation. Now there was just a cold and guarded barrier. "Don't know what you're talkin' about." He picked up another box from the ground, then put it on top of the rest that sat on the palette held by the fork-lift.

Alex had expected this kind of answer. With people like him, there was no point in pussyfooting around and being polite. "Funny, your pal Doug Clegg knew exactly what I was talking about."

"Don't know 'im either." Etchison picked up another case.

"Sure you do." She couldn't help but smile. Despite the incredible frustration men like Etchison inspired within her, Alex found this kind of exchange amusing. "Middle-aged guy? Runs a pawn shop? Ratted you out at a hint of a lawsuit? Dropped any thoughts of suing us when he heard it killed someone? Then showed me the receipt with your signature?"

Etchison released his grip on the case, and spun around to face her, making sure no one else was eavesdropping on them.

"Alright, what's the deal?" he snarled. "You a cop?"

"A cop? No. And I'm more than happy to keep them out of this if you tell me exactly where you got it from."

With a sigh, he glanced around. He couldn't let anyone hear him. Taking a step closer, he lowered his voice. "Outta that statue. The one that crushed the guy. You musta seen it on the news. Huge son of a bitch thing. Squashed the poor bastard flat. No-one knew it was there. No-one missed it. No-one even cared."

This sounded familiar to her. If it was the story she recalled, then she knew the collector well. "You're talking about the Beaumont piece?"

Etchison looked at her blankly.

"Anthony Beaumont? The art collector? His statue? Last week?"

The worker shrugged, then forgot to keep his voice hushed. "How the hell do I know? There was a suit here who'd bought it for a fuckload of cash. Looked like an uppity piece of shit to me. Ain't no clue what his name was."

Nodding a dismissive thanks, Alex turned and started to leave.

"Hey!" he said. Alex glanced back around. "Clegg gave me five hundred bucks for it. Said he overpaid me."

Her smirk returned. She said, "He told us that too, so what?"

"So, did I get fucked?"

Alex turned away again as she answered him clearly. "Royally fucked."


In the midday sun, the Medical School grounds were mostly empty of their normal bustling. With classes still in session, there were barely any students available to take in the warmth of the unseasonably warm weather.

Down the path headed toward the department building, dressed in familiar dumpster-chic, a dark figure walked in the shadows.

A solitary passing student glanced its way, gasping in shock as she caught a glimpse of the figure's distorted features hiding below its hat. She hurried on. The figure didn't break its stride.

Through the otherwise calm weather, a gust of wind blew past the student, following the figure, blowing leaves off its path, clearing its way. Even the branches rustled as it passed underneath them, as if the elements themselves now served the creature in fear.

After walking up the steps to the building, the figure in the tatty garments glanced at the list of department and room numbers printed on the sign affixed to the front door. A blackened, seemingly rotten finger poked out from a ripped glove, traced its way down the listing until it reached the one it was looking for: *ANATOMICAL STUDIES, ROOM 302.*

# CHAPTER
# TEN

Behind huge, ornate metal gates, far up a long driveway, hidden from view by large thick trees, sat the Beaumont mansion. Though located right in the heart of the city, it was not a place many people realized existed. All they saw were the huge gates if they happened to drive by, but with its large walls blocking the view, it drew little attention. A hidden gem within an already exclusive part of town.

The house was so expansive, in fact, that it had its own reception room. Within that room, Alex sat in a Louis XIV chair. It was not the first time she had been here, but as with every visit, she sat in awe. Surrounded by countless works of art, each priceless, she had trouble not looking at them with her mouth agape; from the far wall where the floor-to-ceiling library held countless volumes of antiquarian literature, to the paintings which decorated the walls, all by the masters. She even swore that one of the impressionist classics by the entrance was currently hanging in the Louvre - how was it *here*? No matter how many times she saw this collection it never failed to astonish her.

In her lap sat a newspaper, which had been left casually open on Beaumont's side table; specifically open to an article regarding the accident at the docks. As Beaumont had left her waiting for nearly twenty minutes, she'd had enough time to read the piece a few times.

Finally walking into the room, Anthony Beaumont strode over to Alex with a smile on his face. "My dear Alexandra, how nice to see you again." Moving to stand, Alex sat back down again when her host quickly insisted, "Sit, please. No need to stand on ceremony."

"Mr. Beaumont, I'm so sorry to hear about what happened," she said as she motioned to the newspaper, before closing it and returning it to the side table.

Taking a leather chair opposite, Beaumont smiled thinly. "Yes. Totally irreplaceable you know. One of a kind in every way imaginable."

Alex knew better, "We're talking about your assistant, right? Ed Finney?"

Smooth as silk Beaumont smiled, "Yes, of course." Not missing a beat.

*Liar*, Alex thought. But she did not expect any less. She had dealt with this man on many occasions. Whether selling him some antiquity or appraising some purchase for the insurance coverage, she enjoyed a working relationship with him, but would never accuse him of anything so trivial as human warmth. What he lacked in actual art history knowledge he made up for in his coldness toward people. Though he was always effusive when it came to her.

"Now how can I help my favorite appraiser?" he said.

"If it's not too much of a hard time with your grief, I wonder if I could ask you about the sculpture itself?" She knew full well that he didn't care for the loss of Finney in the slightest. He was probably even a bit happy to have saved money from not having to pay his salary anymore. And he knew she knew this. But they had to play this game, nonetheless.

"Ask me anything you like," he said. He might be angry that he'd lost a valuable item from his collection, and prefer to never think about the statue again, but one thing he did always appreciate was his conversations with Alex.

"The newspaper seemed more concerned with the details of the accident," she said, as reverently as she could. "Dwelling on aspects like the crane operator and such - but even less with—"

"What a drunken swine," he said, cutting in. "A damn hangover! That's what cost me a piece I've been..." Letting the sentiment and attitude trail off, he instead smiled and continued pleasantly. "So, what aspect do you wish to know about?"

"Well, we're given very few details about the statue *itself*. That's what I am interested in."

"I expected no less from you."

"Can you tell me if it was bejeweled?"

"Bejeweled?" A surprising question he had not anticipated. "No. Plain terracotta. Undecorated."

In turn, Alex had not expected to hear that. This did not account for the presence of the opal.

"It was a likeness of Ahura-Mazda," he said, clearly loving the sound of his own voice. "One of the very few to have been made after the Islamic Conversion, and the only one to have survived. Well, for a time, anyway."

"It was in one piece? Before the accident, I mean?"

"Yes. Immaculate condition as well. Locked in a crypt underneath the royal palace for centuries."

"Wow." Under normal circumstances, she would have had to fake this kind of reaction to Beaumont's subtle bragging, but this time she didn't need to. She knew the almost impossibility of the survival of such a piece throughout its country's tumultuous history.

"It would have been a stunning addition to my forgotten Gods collection," he said.

"Your what now?"

Beaumont smiled. "Here." He stood up from his chair. "Let me show you."


Outside Room 302 of the School of Medicine, Charlie Villaraponster - a medical student - approached the door. Pale, slight and in his early twenties, he had the demeanor of someone who was focused solely on his education. It was why he had arrived at his anatomy class twenty minutes early, giving him enough time to prepare. Unlike all of his other classmates, he had not gone to the party last night. No. He was here to study and *only* study.

As he put his hand on the door, he scowled - the way he did every day - at the message underneath the official sign that stated 302: ANATOMICAL STUDIES. It was a handwritten piece of paper, scotch taped to the window; *Dead guys do it with their eyes closed...* and in a different hand, an addition beneath it; *(sometimes)*. He didn't smirk at the joke, but rather at how his classmates seemed intent on mocking the institution they paid to be part of. He disliked them all.

Walking into the darkened room, the only light spilled in from the hallway behind him, but it was enough to show that the room was large and antiseptically clean. Well, as antiseptic as it could be, being a room that contained numerous corpses laid out on slabs - all recently placed there, ready for his class of scalpel wielding sophomores.

Toward the back of the room, in the thick shadows, a figure draped in rags stood hunched over one of the corpses.

Without noticing this interloper, Charlie flipped on the light switch, flooding the room with fluorescent light. That's when he saw the figure.

"Hey! Who are you?" Charlie shouted out. "What are you doing?"

In order to get a clearer view of this stranger, Charlie walked forward and around some tables. As he got closer, a stench hit his nostrils. Not the normal smell of embalming fluid which permeated the cadavers, but a stench of death which rose off this figure like steam.

Charlie came to a sudden stop.

The figure did not answer Charlie's questions, nor did it even react to the new light above. Instead, it continued to lean over the corpse, its claw-like fingernails cutting around the skin of the face as it peeled the skin away with its other hand. Its blackened nails traced a specific pattern of mutilation, so expertly it seemed almost ritualistic in its movements.

"What the fuck?" Charlie said, as he witnessed the figure ripping the fleshy mask free from the glutinous muscle and sinew.

Now holding it in one piece, the dark figure stood and turned to face Charlie.

Its visage now clear, the figure was a vision of corruption. Its flesh was dark and solid with intricate markings decorating every inch of its body. Its eyes were shallow pits that glinted with inhuman knowledge and unholy malice; its lips and jaw swollen as if straining to cover its fang-filled maw.

In its claw-like hand, the figure held up the face it had just stripped from the cadaver. Congealed blood dripped from it, and onto the cold white tile of the floor. The figure's own face creased into a cruel smile of dark amusement at the sight of the student's terror.

Too afraid to run, too afraid to talk, Charlie could only watch, wide-eyed. He did not notice the urine which flowed freely down the inside of his trousers. The figure, though, did and grinned wider.

"Aaaam Iiiii to underssssstand that thisss is something you wish *not* to witness?" the dark figure said with sickly glee. With each word it spoke, its speech became less sibilant, and fuller in form.

With seemingly no control of his faculties, all Charlie could do was nod his head, in a half-paralyzed reply.

"As you wish."

And just like that, Charlie let out a sudden scream. Simultaneously, both of his eyeballs drained of color and solidified. Atom by atom they lost their flesh and attached to the skull in which they sat, becoming one with the bone itself. The student's lids now blinked terrified over the solid form of what had once been his eyes.

The figure smiled at his handiwork.

"*Help me!*" Charlie screamed, his voice an agonized torment, as he staggered in blind shock, swinging wildly about the world of surreal darkness into which he was now condemned.

The figure stepped forward, inhaling deeply. Though the student wore a cologne with an overpowering musk, it could not drown out the smell of fear which dripped from his pores. A scent the figure relished in all of his victims. "I am afraid that there isssss a charge for that wissssh. But, still, let's worry about that when the time comes, shall we?"

The figure then lifted the bloody face it had just removed from the corpse, and layed it over its own. Its hands pressed every square inch of the flayed skin close. The curved edges carved into the skin had been specifically patterned to match the outline of the figure's own visage - expertly and exactly cut to fit over every protuberance he naturally possessed. Swiftly, and with a hidden and terrible magic, this stolen skin fused and sealed itself into place.

The grotesque ugliness of the figure became that of a darkly handsome man. And with this transformation complete, the illusion concealed every last monstrous part of the figure. Now there stood a good-looking man, with mischievous and intelligent eyes. A perfect guise of humanity for a creature so foul.

With a sudden burst of perverse amusement, this monster caught his reflection in a mirror. "A pleasure to meet you," he said.

Alex was in a long gallery-style room in which the walls and alcoves had been adorned with paintings and sculptures depicting ancient gods and goddesses from various countries and faiths - Greek; Roman; Aztec; Celtic; Babylonian - none instantly recognizable. Some carried a powerful and regal air, but others looked twisted and terrifying in their countenances.

She had collapsed in the middle of this room. Coming out of unconsciousness, her eyelids flickered. A concerned and flustered Beaumont kneeled over her with his hand beneath her neck, holding her in a semi-seated position.

"Alexandra, can you hear me? Alex?"

As she started to return to her world, all she could do was let out a blood-curdling scream.

She did not see Beaumont as he was. It might have been his body, but it certainly was not his face. What she saw was the stolen face that the dark, mysterious figure now wore over his own monstrous features. Despite the mask, the creature smiled the same sickly smile.

"Alexandra? What's the matter?" Beaumont said, panicked. This was not something he was used to doing. He would normally have hired help to handle these things - but the hired help had been crushed by nearly half a ton of terracotta and wood.

Alex's vision soon started to clear and she saw Beaumont's face regain its rightful place. The grinning face she'd seen before, at last, faded completely.

"I'm sorry," she slurred as she tried to summon strength. "I... I must have fainted."

With Beaumont's aid, she staggered slowly to her feet.

Trying to keep her steady, she pushed his arm away gracefully. Standing upright, she took a deep breath in. The stink of the figure from her violent vision was now replaced by the musty, familiar air of the mansion.

"Can I get you something? A glass of water, perhaps?"

"No, thank you. I'm okay, really." The last word trailed off as she started noticing details about the room in which she now found herself standing. She had collapsed before she had taken in any of its details. "Wow."

"Alex," Beaumont said. "Please. Are you okay?"

"Yes. Sorry. Must be low blood sugar or something," she lied. "I feel fine. These things come and go. What is this room? It's...incredible."

Smiling, Beaumont accepted this sudden shift to normality after the chaotic panic from a few minutes ago.

He swept his arm theatrically, gesturing about the room. "This is my room of Lost Gods. Beings once worshipped, now mostly forgotten." Turning, he took in the sight of his collection and smiled. "This collection is normally reserved for my own pleasure, but I thought you would have a deep appreciation for it. There is something from most cultures of the ancient world. And down there," he said as he motioned to an empty alcove at the end of the room, "that was where Ahura-Mazda was to have been placed."

"Who *was* Ahura-Mazda?" she asked as she glanced around the room at some of the more obscure sculptures. Some cat-like, some with tentacles, all beautiful, even if terrifyingly so. "What religion?"

"It is only the objects I collect, Alex. Not the theologies they represent, so I am far from an expert."

She knew that was an understatement.

He continued. "But from what I have come to learn, he was a monotheistic deity of the Zoroastrian religion."

"Benevolent?"

"Certainly so. Though what is interesting in his case was that the...opposing force, shall we say, was his own shadow. So, in many respects he himself was the source of the evil he sought to battle."

Alex understood. "A god of good that was also evil? That's deep even for archaic theologies."

"There is someone at the university I can put you in touch with. Very smart woman. I've had her write catalogue descriptions for me previously. Like you, she is indispensable to my collection. You should find her most useful - provided you catch her in a good mood."

Nodding, Alex stared more intently at the room and its contents. As she did, Beaumont's eyes left his collection and followed her instead. Subtly of course. He liked what he saw, physically and mentally. But as he saw her as being so far beneath his class, it was satisfying enough just playing out the mental fantasy.

"You are coming to my party, I hope? It was to be the

unveiling of my new acquisition and to introduce this collection to everyone, but even without Ahura-Mazda, there is still more than enough for people to marvel at. Your employer - Nicholas Merritt - has the invitations. You are more than welcome. It is a plus one as well, should you wish?"

"I might be busy," she said. Not as a brush off, as she did not know where her investigation would take her. "I'd like to, though. I could bring my sister."

"Marvelous."

She looked around the room again. Gods of good and evil. And in the case of the statue with the opal, it seemed to be a God of good *containing* an evil.

She had to fight to push away the newest images she had just witnessed.

She had to remain strong.

*She had to.*

# The Reality of Myth

CHAPTER

# ELEVEN

In the large open-air arena of Kingsworth University, a site traditionally used for team events and concerts, there was a hive of activity that pertained to neither. Students and staff were preparing a large central stage for a new play. At either side of the stage, two huge banners were draped down from the lighting rig which hung high above. They both boldly stated: *CREATION MYTHS - The real history of fake history.*

On the stage, people buzzed around, moving props of all sizes. At the back of the stage, a group of masked students rehearsed their dance moves.

Professor Wendy Derleth - British, vigorous, in her fifties, intense, and with an air of self-assurance that some found vain - stood rigid in front of them. She watched each and every move these students made like a hawk.

"As one! *As one*!" she shouted. "You look like you're all having random seizures!" Without stopping, they continued to repeat the same moves as before, but now trying to focus more.

"Professor Derleth?" A voice interrupted her

concentration. Turning, she saw Alex walk up the steps and onto the stage. "Do you have a moment to talk?"

Rolling her eyes, Wendy replied, "Hold on," before quickly turning back to her students. "Further back. At least ten yards. If you keep starting from this far forward, you'll end up arse first in the orchestra pit!"

Turning back, she smiled, with a pretense of politeness, to her visitor. "Can I help you, Miss...?"

"Amberson. Alex Amberson," Alex said, "And I hope so. I understand Anthony Beaumont called you about me?"

Annoyed, Derleth narrowed her eyes. "Yes. What an insufferable prick that man is. I hope you are less of one."

Alex did not expect this kind of discourse, "Oh, I hope not. I think I can be suffered quite happily."

With a small, genuine smile breaking through the fake polite one, Wendy decided she already quite liked this woman. "Oh, don't worry. It's hardly your problem. Unless you're stupid enough to be working for him, then I take back my feelings that we will get along."

Smiling, Alex shook her head.

"Or sleeping with him? Please tell me no."

"Oh, God no. I have *some* basic standards."

Wendy barked a laugh at Alex's apparent disgust. "Good, well that establishes your discerning taste, at least." Even as she spoke, her eyes trailed across to a student setting down a large throne prop in the middle of the stage. Gesticulating wildly at him, she silently directed him to move the throne to the back of the stage. She continued talking despite her distraction, "So, what is it that I can do for you? Beaumont was not entirely forthcoming, as ever." She turned again, shouting at the student with the throne. "At the fucking back! Is it so hard to understand?!"

The student looked petrified.

Alex, feeling a bit testy - which wasn't entirely the fault of this professor - couldn't help but speak her mind. "You can do nothing at all for me, unless you show me a little respect and give me your attention."

Shocked, Wendy turned back, stared at Alex for a moment, then fully smiled. "Oh, I like you alright. Let's walk. I'm only interfering here, anyway. Something I am remarkably good at, by the way."

They both descended the stairs. Wendy continued. "This is a co-production. Folklore Department, that's me. And Theater Arts. That's not. As soon as Doctor Campbell gets here, I'd be asked to leave, anyway. I have a knack of speaking my mind, you see. And none of these prissy actor types appreciate that. You seem to be a woman after my own heart."

A few minutes later, walking in the gardens of the university grounds, Wendy listened attentively as Alex shared her story.

"An opal buried in Ahura-Mazda?" Wendy asked. "Hmm, it rings a bell, I think."

"Yeah?" Alex asked.

"Stone of the Secret Fire, I think. A legend. At least that's my recollection of the name. It's just a myth, of course. You have to understand, none of us actually *believe* this stuff. We study it for what it tells us about the human condition and historical context, not for signposts to the supernatural."

"Supernatural or not," Alex said, "I can tell you that the opal was real. I saw it. I touched it."

"Oh, I don't doubt that." Wendy stopped and caught Alex's gaze. "It was of course real, and within that very statue undoubtedly. I am just saying it is fascinating the lengths the priests went to, just to lend credence to their silly stories. I very much doubt any of them believed what they peddled."

"And what was this story? Did it say what the stone was?"

Wendy and Alex continued to walk around the gardens. As they approached the main building, more and more students emptied from classes and milled about the area. But the students did not pay any attention to Wendy or Alex, they just went about their day, in their own worlds.

"The Stone of the Secret Fire, or Jewel of the Secret Fire, I can't remember which. Well, it was first written about in Persia, nearly nine hundred years ago. It was a beautiful fire-red opal - as you described. A court Sorcerer was said to have imprisoned an evil spirit, or entity, within it."

"An evil spirit?" Alex asked.

"A creature from the spaces between the worlds. A Djinn." Wendy smiled as she said the next words. "A genie to most people."

Alex glanced at Wendy as if about to burst out laughing.

"I know, I know. It's ludicrous. But clear your mind of what our culture has made of the Djinn. Forget Barbara Eden, forget Robin Williams. For the people of the ancient Arabian lands, a Djinn was neither cute, nor funny. It was, to them, something else entirely. Something that they dreaded to be set free. It was the face of fear itself. "

A young sales assistant, Ariella, stood waiting outside the changing room of a high-end clothing store. Trying to remain patient, she could not help but glance at her watch. *How long is he going to take?* she thought to herself. She had been waiting here for quite some time.

A customer walked by. Ariella offered the customer her

scripted "*Good afternoon.*" The customer looked her up and down as if Ariella were a side of bacon.

*Good afternoon. Urgh.*

Something her boss made sure employees said to *every* customer they saw. No matter who they were.

*Always a greeting of the time of day. No exceptions. No excuses. Every customer is your better and should be treated as such.*

That would be fine, but a large percentage of the customers were just collectively rude, abusive assholes. Men who thought her eyes were in her chest, and barely ever broke that eye contact, and women who looked at her like she had just smeared shit on their favorite linens. She wasn't from this part of town. She wasn't well-to-do. She couldn't even afford a pair of the cheapest cufflinks that were sold here. Though she was proud that she could scrub up well enough to at least exist in the peripheries of this world; all part of her plan to get what she wanted.

This job was just a necessary stepping-stone. She needed money. She had a future to prepare for, after all. So, she would suck up the bullshit for yet another day. Wait on another customer taking their sweet-ass time.

Well, she didn't mind this one. The one in the dressing room she stood waiting for. There was something about him. Something... enticing. Even though he had looked at her like a lion sizing up a gazelle.

"How does it look, sir?" she finally called, back over the curtain, to the man changing inside. *He must have it on by now.*

The curtain immediately swung back, as if on cue, and the Djinn walked out. Complementing his borrowed human face, the Djinn wore an incredibly well-fitting suit, a finely pressed shirt, and shoes that you could see your reflection in.

Dressed to kill, she thought.

"You tell me," he said.

His voice now held none of the demonic tone it carried before. The guttural malice now replaced with a smooth, bassy tone. A pleasing sound, though still laced with mischief.

Ariella let slip a "Nice!". But it was not merely a placatory lie to sell an overpriced bundle of cotton to a dumbass with more money than sense. This suit did indeed elevate this man's look, as if it were somehow tailored specifically for him.

"I'm glad you approve." He smiled, and his sharp, blackened teeth were transformed, by illusion, to a bright set of pearly whites. And, using the same magic, his body no longer looked monstrous, but instead toned and slim.

"Would you like to try another style? Tighter maybe?" This suit *was* perfect for him, but she *had* to try to sell him more. It *was* her job, after all.

"Tighter?" he said, rhetorically. "No, I do not think so. I do not like to be confined any more than I have to. I have had enough of that."

"Okay then," she smiled. "Follow me."

"With pleasure."

As she turned and walked to the register, she could feel - and was not unhappy about - his eyes on her. Sometimes the ogling was actually enjoyable, when it came from the right person. And this man - with his mesmeric stare - was definitely the right kind of person.

Walking behind the counter to the cash register, she looked up at the man, maintaining her smile. "So will this be cash or charge, Mr....?"

The Djinn thought for a moment, before exhaling with a smile. "Demarest. Nathaniel Demarest. Please, call me Nathaniel."

"Okay, Nathaniel. Cash or charge?"

"Which would you prefer?"

Ariella giggled. "I don't mind. Cash?"

"And how much of it would you like?" The words spilled over his stolen lips as his eyes locked with hers.

"Nine hundred seventeen dollars and eighty-seven cents. Including tax."

"You misunderstand me," he said as he took a step nearer to the counter. "How much... would you *like*?"

His manner seemed flirtatious and well-meaning, though his intentions were anything but. Ariella however, was happy to play along, blind to the reality of the situation.

"Call it an even thousand. Don't wanna be greedy after all."

With a slow blink, this pretender calling himself Nathaniel Demarest spoke the words he always lusted to say...

"As you wish."

As the words were spoken, a hush fell over the store.

She felt a sudden bulge, as something moved in her blouse pocket. She fished her hand inside and brought out a bundle of cash. A thousand dollars to be precise. Looking at it with wonder, then to Demarest, she struggled with the words. "My God. How... How did you?"

Lifting his finger to his gleeful lips, "Shhhh. It's a kind of magic."

She didn't know what to say. What to do. Astonishment clouded her thoughts. How did the money get there? It wasn't like she'd felt him touch her or anything.

And right at this moment, she *wanted* him to touch her.

"Now, Ariella, would you be interested in any further transactions?"

If she has been thinking more clearly, she would have remembered that her name badge only had her first initial and last name on it. Nowhere was her first name available for this man to see.

Shrugging, her eyes sparkled as she looked into his eyes. She was certain this strange and beautiful man - probably two decades older than her at least - was about to ask her out.

"You are a very beautiful woman," he said.

She now knew *for sure* a date would be certainly proffered next.

"Ariella. Very beautiful. Tell me, does it trouble you to know that your beauty will someday fade? That your looking-glass will day by day remind you that your flesh is created only to rot and wither? Your life, only a long story with an unhappy ending?"

This was not the proposal she was expecting.

"I... I mean... That's life, right?," she said, forcing a laugh. "Happens to us all."

"Not *all* of us." he said. His stare grew more intent, hungrier, with each passing moment. "Try it, young Ariella. *Ask*. Ask and see what happens. Ask for an end to change, and an end to decay. An end to the inevitable atrophy of your flesh-bound existence. Usually I only give one wish away. But to you, I can make an exception as you assisted me in choosing this fine suit."

She was at a loss for words. *What was this guy talking about?*

His voice now almost a whisper, he looked away for a moment at the other customers milling around, and then back to her - locking his gaze deep into hers. "Say, 'I wish to be beautiful, forever.'"

Almost as though hypnotized, she did as this man asked. "I wish to be beautiful forever."

A wicked smirk crossed his face.

"As you wish. A pleasure doing business with you, Ariella."


Walking through the large main foyer of the store, Demarest held his head high as he approached the exit. He opened one of the oversized glass doors, then paused as he held it open for a short, stout, elderly lady who walked inside with a smile.

"Thank you, young man," she said with a happy croak, "It's not often you see old-world courtesy these days."

Bowing his head, Demarest smiled in acknowledgement. Old-world? *How little this infant knew.*

Walking over to the register, the elderly woman pulled out a shawl from her handbag, ready to make a return on her purchase. A thing she did often, even if against store policy, for no one ever refused someone her age.

As she reached the counter, she looked around, annoyed. There were no staff here. Strange. Normally they were ready to assist at any given moment. She waddled away, annoyed that she had to find someone herself.

Behind the counter stood five mannequins, beautifully dressed in the latest fashions currently available for sale. All except one: the female one at the front - the one that took up most of the space behind the counter. An exquisitely beautiful mannequin who wore staff clothing donning Ariella's name badge, and in whose blouse pocket sat a bundle of hundred-dollar bills. The mannequin's eyes may have seemed solid and lifeless, but within, they helplessly stared out across the store, trapped in a nightmare wish.

CHAPTER

# TWELVE

"So, slowly, faith becomes myth, then it loses all its—" Wendy Derleth's voice suddenly became edgy with offense, and her eyes narrowed. "Am I boring you? You're the one who asked me about the Djinn."

Alex's sight was lost within the whirl of the newest apparition that had been thrust upon her. Each of these visits to a hellish reality left her weaker and weaker. As she blinked hard, the vision disappeared - and reality flooded back. Gone was the clothing store with the tormented mannequin.

Wendy and Alex sat on benches in the middle row of the arena's seating area. Below them, the staging was still being set up, the performers still practicing their moves. For the first time since she had suffered from these visions, Alex had somehow managed to keep conscious. If she hadn't, Wendy may have noticed. Though she had been so caught up in her storytelling she hadn't even seen Alex's head lolling back as she was stolen away to witness the Djinn's evil once again.

"Alex?" Wendy said with a stern snap. "Are you even listening to me?"

Regaining some grip on herself, Alex replied "I... I'm sorry.

I am listening." She tried her best to cover up her nausea, and gather her thoughts as her mind swam with a rising panic.

"Well, I am damn close to boring myself," Wendy said, not entirely convinced. She got to her feet. "Wait here."

Wendy strode across the field toward a fold-out table, where students dispensed coffee for the gathered performers and workers. The queue was long, and the students who were serving frantically tried to keep up with the orders. The cash box that sat on the table overflowed with dollar bills. Wendy, being the bullish professor she was, cut the line and walked straight to the front. Nobody uttered a word of protest. They wouldn't dream of saying *anything* to rile her.

Alex took a deep breath and closed her eyes for a moment.

"What the hell is going on?" Alex said quietly to herself. Her thoughts swelled with a multitude of possible rational explanations and malignant illnesses to explain her condition. But she found herself focusing on the terrifying idea that a tumor was currently devouring her brain and causing her to suffer these hellish visions. Yet despite this, something ineffable, something deep within her, was stopping her from truly believing this was anything but real, and that there was no illness at play.

That face she saw in the glimpses. That terrible face. That voice. Both now changed, but somehow the same. Everything about these experiences told her *something* was very wrong.

Opening her eyes again, she glanced at the rows upon rows of empty seating, the sun high in the sky gracing another day of pleasant spring weather. Standing, she took a blind step sideways, and all but collided into a robed figure with a twisted demonic face.

Alex screamed.

The student in front of her removed the demon mask he wore, and looked suitably terrified, and apologetic.

"Oh jeez, I'm so sorry lady," the student said, fumbling over his words. "I thought you were Professor Derleth. I can't really see much in this thing." He motioned to the mask in his hands.

Alex regained her composure and swallowed hard. If she thought she had high blood pressure before, it was nothing compared to now.

"I wanted her to check the costume out," the student said.

Arriving behind him with two cups of dishwater colored coffee in her hands, Wendy shook her head at the student.

"Well obviously it's scary enough. Now get back to rehearsal." She handed Alex one of the cups. "Black, no sugar. Sorry, I forgot to ask how you take it." She noticed the student was still standing nearby, frozen in an awkward stance. He was clearly still in shock from his encounter with Alex. "Well? Get going then?" she said, waving her free hand at him.

With this, he finally scampered off, tail between his legs, and said "I'm sorry" again.

Alex, feeling very self-conscious, sipped her coffee, then smiled at Wendy. "It's perfect, thank you."

It was, of course, far from perfect. But it was warm and soothing, which would do.

Wendy regarded Alex for a moment as they both took sips of their bitter drinks. Wendy noticed how Alex was perspiring and had a slight tremble to her hands. "Perhaps we should do this another time, when you are feeling more up to it?"

"You might think me crazy, but time isn't something I'm sure there's an abundance of," she said with a look of defeat, "Please, tell me more about the Djinn."

"If you're sure?"

Alex nodded and took another sip; getting used to its unappealing taste.

"Well, the word, Djinn, is both singular and plural, by the

way. Various cultures believe they are a powerful and magical race of beings."

"Are you saying this as fact?" Alex asked, not realizing her words could easily be interpreted as sarcasm.

"Of course not!" Wendy said. "Legend says they were created by God after the angels but before mankind. They were the Yin to the angels' Yang. All creation is about balance, according to folklore. When the angels were created good and benevolent, an opposite had to be created to balance the scales. An opposite as evil and malevolent as the angels were holy. As the myth asserts, anyway."

Alex wondered how she got to be here, chasing down the history of a stone. How ridiculous it was. Then the image of Josh, lying dead on the science lab floor, hit her again.

Wendy continued. "The Djinn, as they were all about destruction, were never given a real home by the creator, which is understandable really, and supposedly pissed them off to no end. This anger twisted their entire focus toward punishing their creator by destroying His other creations."

"Like devils, basically?" asked Alex.

"Devils, demons, all part of the same myth after it had been retold by Abrahamic lenses."

"So where does the genie thing come into it? They granted wishes, right?"

"They are obliged to. Their Creator foresaw what they were capable of, so cursed them by forcing them to do what humanity asked by granting three wishes for every person who summoned them. This backfired, though."

"Backfired?"

"Apparently, when the Creator cast them to the void in the first place, He knew they would have a way into our world after humans called them with their magic. So, as a failsafe, after the djinn were obliged to grant the wishes, they would be forced to return to the void. A kind of 'fuck you' to their kind."

"Why three wishes? Seems a bit random."

"Three being the holy number. The Trinity. Always in threes, in these tales. The idea was they would have to serve that which they despised before having to return to the void. That void, though, had an effect even the creator didn't foresee."

"Not an infallible God, then?" Alex smirked.

Wendy, took another sip of the coffee, and said, "These tales were written throughout many centuries, over and over again by many different holy men and religions, so don't expect an airtight plotline."

"Over the centuries," Wendy continued, "legends become fairy tales. We avoided the terrors in the night by inventing stories of magical lamps."

"So that's not the truth?"

"Alex, again, *none* of this is true. All tales were told by ignorant minds. Don't get confused. Just because the stories are old doesn't mean they're any more real than the promises politicians break on a daily basis. They are to be taken as fiction only, even if some have a small basis in fact."

"Very dark fables. Gotcha." Alex nodded. "So, how does this link to the sorcerer putting the opal in the statue?"

"Let me continue," Wendy said, curtly. She hated interruptions. "During their eternity in the void, the Djinn grew more twisted and more powerful, and they used the curse to their advantage. The wishes became punishments as they twisted the wishes' meanings to their own needs. And as angels were made to fuel themselves on life itself, the Djinn had to conversely feed on death... meaning their curse also ended up making them stronger. With each wish, they ate some of the wisher's soul, so when they departed, they only left destruction. So, as you said, not the most infallible God making that a possibility. And it went on and on like this for eons. One by one, the Djinn were called by man. Who then gave them three wishes, and went back when done. But as time passed, the wishes became punishments. Then... things changed again."

"Changed?"

"Apparently the Djinn grew tired, and one by one retreated deeper into the void; leaving only one to be called. One who wanted more than anything to usurp man's stronghold on this planet. And it planned to free its brothers forever from the void's shackles. One story says it made a bargain with a warlock to imbue it with powers to break through the veil between existences so it might release the rest of the Djinn onto earth."

"Why would a Djinn make a bargain with anyone?"

"The warlock was, as the story goes, the only person who ever encountered a Djinn and saw it for what it was. Saw beyond the illusions. So he made the Djinn an offer. He would use his magics to aid the Djinn, and in return the warlock asked for three wishes with no ironic repercussions. Anyway, the warlock could not undo God's will, He could only adjust it, and made it so that the Djinn could grant wishes to *anyone*, rather than just the person that called it from the void.

"Though in folklore, all magic has consequences. And so with this bargain, the Djinn would be able to feed on more souls which enabled it to become stronger and stronger in our world. So, sure, whenever the Djinn eventually granted the three wishes of its summoner, the void would once again open, to send it back. But the only problem is, if the Djinn had enough power, it could try to not only stay here, but pull others of its kind into our world. And none of those new Djinn would be beholden to wishes. Then again, this is just my understanding of a myth, which is pure fiction, anyway; so take my half-remembered retelling of this made-up story with a grain of salt." Wendy laughed.

"And the opal?"

"I'm getting to that," Wendy said. "So there was a king, some say Persian, some Mesopotamian, depending on the texts. But this king summoned it, and sure as the warlock had enabled it to, the Djinn fed - one by one - on the people in the city, before gaining immense strength and power, and then finally offering the king his three wishes; each one a worse punishment than the last, twisting the king's words to fit into the creature's own perverted needs. But before the king could complete a final wish, his sorcerer cast the djinn into what they called *the Stone of the Secret Fire*. Which made me think of the opal you mention. So it stands to reason that there would be a statue of Ahura-Mazda which, symbolically, due to what it was supposed to be, could have had a red gemstone hidden within it to represent the darkness within the divinity. But all folklore is a jumbled mess of a thousand stories meshed into one diluted parable."

"Where was the stone from? Do any of the texts say?"

"Nothing that I remember."

Piece by piece, the links between the story and the statue started to become clearer to Alex. They even somewhat explained that troubling nebula within the center of the gem.

Alex had all-but-officially lost faith in her hopeful brain tumor theory.

CHAPTER

# THIRTEEN

The first-floor open-plan office of the overworked police station bustled with life. At desks that littered the room, cops interviewed witnesses, and booked suspects; all part of the normal day at this precinct in the busy metropolitan city. The fact no one was screaming or fighting in here was a welcome respite, as these were not only daily occurrences here, but almost hourly.

Detective Nathanson sat at his desk. He rubbed an eye with the palm of his hand. In front of him lay the folder covering the Joshua Aickman accident. The photos of the scene proved difficult viewing. Close-up images of the seared wounds on the corpse stayed in the detective's mind long after he looked away from them. But he couldn't complain. This was what he'd signed up for. This was what he had trained for. This was what he had to prove he was *made* for.

After looking over everything, he was confident the case had been an accident. He was ready to finish his report, and close the case.

"Detective?" a smooth, low voice said, breaking into Nathanson's thoughts.

Looking up, Nathanson saw a finely-suited man approaching his desk. As the stranger approached, the detective guessed the man was in his late forties.

"Nathaniel Demarest," the stranger said, and smiled like a Cheshire Cat. "Your colleagues downstairs informed me that it was you who is in charge of the investigation at the school. The accident in the lab."

"Yes." Nathanson smiled weakly and nodded, motioning to the seat in front of his desk. "Please, sit." He glanced at the Aickman file as though it were taunting him, then sighed, hoping this stranger wasn't here to change his mind.

Demarest sat down. "I hope I have not caught you at a bad moment?"

"Not at all," he lied. "So, the Aickman accident. That case is now closed, as far as Homicide is concerned, but-"

"That is very pleasing to know," Demarest said, interrupting.

"Yeah. And as I was gonna say, though I would like to assist, I think you would do better talking to someone in a more suitable department. Unless you have something to say which is relevant to the Homicide department?"

"Actually," Demarest said, never dropping the smile, "I was hoping you had something for *me*."

At the desk next to them, two detectives were speaking to a suspect. Their voices had begun to raise and steal away the attention of both Nathan and Demarest for a moment.

"We know you did it," shouted the first detective, losing his patience. "Your bullshit ain't cuttin' it."

"You were there!" said the other, equally agitated.

"I wasn't even in town!" the suspect said, a smarmy smile on his face.

The negative emotions washed over Demarest like warm

spring water. He did so enjoy it when humans turned on one another.

"What do you think I have for you, Mr. Demarest?" Nathanson asked, cutting into the shouting at the next table and regaining Demarest's attention.

"The full name and address of the woman called Alexandra." Demarest leaned forward, closer to the detective, and continued. "I am sure you know of whom I speak." As he talked, he slowly tilted his head toward the shouting officer, to better overhear the interrogation.

"*You sonofabitch, just admit it!*" The first detective again.

"No point lying anymore!"

Demarest noticed that Nathanson was also listening in, while still trying to retain his professionalism.

"Yeah, I know the woman you mean," Nathanson said. "But what in hell makes you think I would ever just hand details like that over to a stranger?"

Demarest pondered this for a moment before replying, "For the satisfaction of a citizen?"

Looking over his own shoulder, Nathanson glanced at the large poster on the wall which boldly stated, *'To protect and to serve, for the satisfaction of our citizens'.*

"Cute," Nathanson replied, unamused. He did not like this guy.

"I didn't do shit!" shouted the suspect.

Nathanson spoke to Demarest, while keeping an eye on the shouting suspect in his periphery. "Now let me ask you something in return. What's your interest in this case? What's your interest in this witness? How did you even—"

"I would be delighted to answer any and all of your queries, " Demarest said, "but please, answer me, why do you keep looking at the other desk?"

As Nathanson answered, he tried to stop himself from

saying too much, but he felt the other detective's frustration. On any other day, he wouldn't dream of telling a stranger - even one he could tell was an asshole from fifty yards - anything about any case. But he couldn't help himself. It was like he *had* to tell someone. "The guy they're talking to is as guilty as sin. Seven counts of murder have been thrown at him over the last two years. Walks every time. Guy's made of Teflon. It makes me sick."

"What would you like to do about it?"

"I'm sorry. I shouldn't be talking about this," Nathanson said, catching himself. "So, as I was saying—"

"*You don't have shit on me!*" the suspect shouted. "So either book me or let me the fuck go!"

Nathanson closed his eyes as he shared in the exasperation of his colleagues.

"Tell me Detective." Demarest spoke in a hushed tone, yet his voice somehow carried loudly to the detective's ears. "In a perfect world, what would you like to happen?"

"I want that prick dead-to-rights," Nathanson said under his breath as he stared at the failing interrogation. "Murder one. Lots of witnesses this time."

Demarest smiled.

"As you wish."

Suddenly, the suspect screamed in a primal fury. Like a man possessed, he leaped across the desk and, before anyone could do anything about it, he grabbed one of the detectives' guns from its holster. The suspect cocked it with a professional ease.

"Jesus!" Nathanson said.

The suspect shot both of his interrogators like a skilled assassin; both in the chest and in the head. It was over before anyone watching could even blink.

The entire station suddenly erupted into pandemonium

at the echoing shots and sprays of blood. Panicked civilians scrambled to escape, forgetting all other concerns.

A few officers drew their weapons to apprehend the suspect, but there were too many people rushing in front of them to give them a clear shot.

Quickly, another detective tackled the suspect to the ground. Another rushed over to pry the stolen gun from his hand. The suspect shots were fired two rounds into the ceiling above before finally being subdued.

Nathanson, like every other policeman in the room, rushed over to assist.

And the second he was gone, Demarest stood up casually and opened the folders on the detective's desk.

Nathanson did not notice as his visitor looked at the file, nor at the business card Demarest removed, which read—

Alexandra Amberson
Buried Treasure Auction House
1001 Shahrazad Dive

"There you are..." Demarest said in his demonic tone, forgetting to use his human voice.

Nathanson looked up then, and he saw Demarest close the file, and pocket the business card. Their eyes locked for a moment.

"Hey!" Nathanson shouted, but before he could alert anyone else to Demarest's actions, the restrained suspect began howling in renewed rage.

With impossible strength, the suspect threw off the policemen who attempted to subdue him. Still clutching the gun he had grabbed, he leveled his aim at those trying to intervene and fired four more times. Four more policemen fell dead. All perfect headshots.

Without a second thought, the rest of the officers and detectives, including Nathanson, drew their guns simultaneously. Their bullets hit their marks, riddling the suspect's body, yet somehow, he remained standing.

"What the fuck's he on, PCP?!" a uniformed officer shouted in the panic.

Before the suspect could turn his gun on them, the officers fired at him again. Each one hitting their marks perfectly, and each wound opening up and jettisoning blood.

Grabbing the nearest cop with one hand, the possessed man hauled the cop off his feet as though the officer weighed nothing.

Everyone ceased fire, out of fear of hitting their captured colleague.

"Put him down!" Nathanson shouted.

The suspect smashed the butt into the officer's face, connected with his jaw. This powerful blow cracked the bone clean from his skull, and the flesh tore around the officer's mouth. Blood gushed freely as his tongue lolled out grotesquely from the wound.

The suspect then let go of his grip, dropping the officer to the floor. The officer lay there, helplessly choking on his own blood in his final moments of life. His jaw hanging from the face, held only by a few strands of still-connected skin.

With a clear shot now available, the surrounding policemen carried on their assault against the suspect. But no matter how many times they shot him - nothing they did seemed to knock him down. Soon enough, they ran out of ammo, and the firing ceased.

Through a smoky haze, they were left staring at the scene

in front of them: the suspect, riddled with dozens of bullet holes over his head and torso, very much alive, breathing in heavy grunts; at his feet, the dead jawless officer.

Suddenly, the suspect jerked his head, and his face twisted in desperate confusion for a moment, as if he'd been recently woken from a nightmare. Then he simply fell to the floor, dead, as if the switch of life had been flipped off.

Their shots had finally taken effect.

Before anyone that was left standing could begin to even figure out what had just happened, Nathanson looked back to his desk.

Demarest was gone.

## CHAPTER
# FOURTEEN

The next day went by in a daze. Alex had finished her conversation with Wendy and gone straight to every library and bookstore she could find, scouring them for more information on the subject of forgotten gods and the Djinn; maxing her credit card to gather all the research she could. She knew she wasn't really crazy. She had seen things that were beyond visions any tumor or madness could create. Even so, she had to cover all bases. Even making a call to the city records library, she grasped at straws for a rational explanation, searching for where the gas mains ran near her house and work, just to be sure there was no other possible explanation.

Now back in her apartment, bathed in the subdued glow of an ornate lamp, she sat at her desk, deeply engrossed in her studies. The dozens of books she had bought were in categorized piles across the floor. Old volumes on folklore lay open at bookmarked pages on the desk. On the wall ahead of her, a corkboard was decorated with pinned photocopied images, drawn symbols, handwritten notes, and ripped out book pages with highlighted passages. These were the keys to her search. The findings of her current obsession.

Her finger trailed down the page of the ornate leather-bound encyclopedia of ancient religions. This oversized tome opened to the page on Middle Eastern deities.

The musty odor of these pages intoxicated her. It was the smell of knowledge. She felt like she was in college again, holed up in a dark corner of the library, reading everything she could on antiquities and history. She felt most alive when lost in the past, something she had not had much of an opportunity for recently. She realized that fictional folklore, a subject she had barely gazed at before, was as engrossing a subject as the factual past. Her studies had always been on provable truths, histories of antiquity - not the stories behind them. And it was the romanticism of these old gods and beliefs that enchanted her, despite the shadow that stood in the corner of her mind. The one that screamed at her to run. To hide. That the Djinn *was* real. That she was in danger.

"The world has no perils to the rage of these orphans of God," Alex read aloud.

She nodded as she considered the words. Turning, she wrote the quote down onto the pad of paper that lay next to her - the scrawl joining the rest of the page's collection, all of which fell under the chapter title of *Quotes about the Djinn*.

Her eyes fed over the next paragraph in this book:


*Though references to the Djinn appear over many texts - including scriptures of the Koran - it is the writings of Abdul Alhazrar that provide most of what we know of these mythical beasts.*

· · ·

Turning the page, her eyes darted over a series of images. The first was a woodcut of villagers cowering from a large, demonic, dark-skinned creature, complete with jagged teeth and an oversized, engorged, threatening penis. The next, a Hieronymus Bosch-type painting of three layers of existence. The top showed the bright sun, angels dancing around it. The middle showed farmers working the land on earth. The bottom was all darkness except for the beasts who stared up angrily - strikingly similar depictions of the beast to the woodcut image. The last image was a photograph of a ritual cloth from a lost African tribe. That, too, depicted a creature in an eerily similar form.

*Religious and non-religious folklore both trace a similar vein of the Djinn. Though referred to by different names, many cultures over many centuries have all shared similar depictions of a beast offering wishes. Note that every image above shares the iconography of the advancing monster with the erect phallus. This is a mere representation of their belief that the Djinn fed on desire. There are no mentions in any found manuscripts which detail the Djinn as having any designated sex. Like angels, they are presumed to be sexless and eternal, without a need for procreation.*

Just below this passage sat a drawing of a jewel. An opal. The same opal Alex once held. The same opal that had something strange hidden within its core.

*With the passage of time, meanings and rituals of beliefs become lost or evolve. The same can be said for the calling of the Djinn. Alhazrar wrote that, over the centuries, the knowledge of how to call forth a Djinn became relegated to necromancers and shamans, until they too faced their own extinction with the advancement of science, effectively trapping the Djinn for eternity in an obscurity. This left the secret of their reality, and passage to the void they dwelled in, known to very few, whereas the stories of their existence were told and retold over time, effectively erasing their original demonic forms, and casting the Djinn into a diluted fairy-tale.*

*The Stone of the Secret Fire was said to be a prison for the last of the Djinn who had not forsaken the earth. It was the most powerful of them; the one who had broken its chains and rebelled against God and man alike. Trapped by a sorcerer into a fire-stone jewel, this creature had to abide by the curse of the creator. A door had to remain; a door upon which man could call forth this creature. Yet unlike before, where the Djinn may be called forth from a fire or the darkness, now it could only be called by the one who found and charged the stone with their lifeforce. Accordingly, this sorcerer hid the mythic jewel, intent that the doorway forever be undiscovered; thus casting this story to absolute myth, the same as with the writings of the Holy Grail from Abrahamic beliefs.*

Alex, hypnotized by the words on the page, did not hear the footsteps outside her apartment. She did not hear the lock turn. She did not hear the door open, or close. She was too lost in the next lines:

*Alhazrar wrote in the last of his texts, one final warning - confirming his belief in the existence of these creatures. Should you call forth a Djinn, you are calling forth your own damnation. There is no escaping the shadow that dwells behind you, with one hand on your shoulder, guiding you to the darkness.*

. . .

As if on cue, a hand touched Alex's shoulder. She screamed and spun on her chair, her eyes wide with expectation that it was the presence in her visions now manifest in front of her - *The Djinn.*

"Whoa!" Shannon said. "Calm down, big sister!"

"Fuck! You scared the hell out of me." The panic subsided. Alex swallowed as her heartbeat slowed. "Everyone seems to be doing this to me recently."

"Didn't you hear me come in?" Shannon said. "I was calling for you." As she spoke, her eyes moved up and she regarded the corkboard, the many pads of scrawled notes, and the books splayed open haphazardly over the desk and floor. "What the hell are you doing? Is this what you have been up to all day?" Her voice had a tinge of worry.

"Learning the rules of the game," Alex said.

Shannon stared for a moment, glanced down to her watch, then back up to her sister, "A different game to the basketball game you should be at?"

*Oh fuck*, Alex thought as she sprang from her chair and grabbed her coat from the back of her chair. "I completely forgot!"

"I had to cover for you. What's happening?" Shannon was worried, though tried to not sound angry. She didn't want a repeat performance of the other night.

"What's...happening?" Alex asked.

"Work? With Nick? Your boss? Christ Alex, you didn't call in and tell them where you were."

"I'm so sorry," Alex said, flustered. "What did you tell Nick?"

"Female problems. You know how squeamish he is. So no questions asked." She sighed, "C'mon, I'll drive you..."

# FIFTEEN

Weaving his way elegantly through a throng of pedestrians, the Djinn, donning his human skin, walked the evening streets. Looking around at the passing masses, he felt like a lion in lamb's wool. He could smell the desperation in them, screaming out at him. He liked this new world. The knowledge he consumed about it - from those he had already slaughtered - filled his mind with wonder and potential. This blossoming world would make a worthy new home to obliterate.

Along with the knowledge stolen from each victim, his power grew and pulsed through him like an approaching storm. Every fiber within him vibrated in anticipation.

As he walked, he grinned, feeling the gaze of several women regarding him with lust in their eyes. He regarded each of them, but none had what he was looking for. One of the women approached and slowed down. As she did, he caught her gaze, and slowed his gait as well. He could sense the moisture emanating from her loins. He could sense her desire. Her eyes regarded him intensely. They were wide. Entranced.

She had no way of knowing that her intoxication was simply an illusion - one that the Djinn exuded - which enchanted its victims, as it drew them in.

He could sense her longing. Her very being would make a marvelous meal, if he had the time.

Had he been created a human, he may have stopped to give in to this woman's desires. But he was not a man - and would sooner mutilate her than pleasure her.

He had no time for either. He had to find the one who called him forth into this world. And when he found *her*, the connection would be made, and she would not be able to escape from him.

Before walking on, Demarest wagged his finger, teasing the woman, and said, "Be careful what you wish for..."

Walking on, he left the woman feeling foolish and confused.

As he walked, he closed his eyes and whispered to himself... "Alexandra..."

He pulled out her business card and smirked. He would keep his destination from her this time. He had given her the gift of witnessing his work through his eyes. Now, however, he wanted his arrival to be a surprise.


Breaking off from her pep talk with the girls of her basketball team, Alex looked around. Had she heard someone call her name? But no one was there. It was only her and the girls in the hall.

The girls looked at each other quizzically, not knowing the answer to the question posed.

"You have to know you can win?" Sierra said, hopeful. Alex snapped back to attention.

"Uh... yeah, exactly." Alex pushed through her

nightmarish thoughts. "You have to *know* you can win. That's the secret no one tells you. Most teams go out either thinking they could lose or praying for a miracle to win. But with thinking like that, the game is already lost. Belief is half the battle." She clapped her hands together. "Now let's get ready for the game, your parents'll be here soon."

As the girls turned and ran away in unison, heading to the changing rooms, Alex took one last look around. She was pretty sure *someone* said her name.

Despite what she had told the girls, she felt like she was playing a game she didn't have any idea *she* could win. After the volumes of research she'd drowned herself in, she was left cold and nervous. She *knew* folklore was fiction and only based on a very loose grasp of the truth, but she had held the opal, had seen inside it. She believed it had power. She had lost hours. She had lost her best friend. She had seen things *impossible* to see, on multiple occasions. All the arrows pointed to these tales containing more truth within them than not. But she was like an ant in an airport. Insignificant and incapable of understanding the halls in which she roamed. If there *was* no Djinn, then why had she been blacking out? Why had she seen visions? Why was all the research starting to make more sense the deeper and deeper she tumbled down the rabbit hole?

From the moment she looked into the opal, she had swung back and forth between blind faith in the mythology, to believing she *was* losing her mind, and back again. Over and over. Shifting between trusting her eyes, to bargaining with her brain. As she stood in the court now, she made a mental note. She needed to see a doctor - maybe even start taking the pills again.

. . .

The upscale shopping street was desolate, the stores now closed for the night; their fronts all darkened and secured.

"We're closed sir," the security guard said in his stern monotone, as he sat at his desk in the foyer of Buried Treasure Auction House. He was speaking to a stranger who tapped on the glass front door vying to get his attention. From his years working the night shift, he was used to the assholes of the city walking by and choosing to bother him. Begging for change. Begging to use the toilets. Always begging for *something*! Rich, poor, white, black, male, female - didn't matter. They always bothered him when he sat for a night shift.

He would, though, not change this for the world. He was in charge here. Sure, the contents of the building may not be his property - but he was responsible for it all. This was *his* dominion to rule with an iron fist. This was where he felt the only power in his life.

So, let them bother him.

Let them tap on the glass.

Let them tell their goddamn sob stories.

They would all get the same rejection from him.

But tonight was not a normal night. Tonight the boss was still here, working late, and the guard's feeling of power was slightly diminished by his presence; especially when he had to help his employer straighten more paintings - even though they were already straight.

That was an hour ago, and he was now back at his desk. He *could* pretend the back of the building didn't exist. That the boss was not there. That he was once again king of the castle.

Another tap on the glass.

The guard furrowed his brow and called out to this interrupter again.

"It's after hours. Come back tomorrow."

Another tap.

*Jeez, this guy isn't lettin' up.*

Getting up from his chair, the guard walked over to the sharply-dressed man standing on the other side of the glass. The guard puffed out his chest to the visitor as he walked, making himself appear as big as he possibly could.

"I am trying to locate one of the employees of this establishment," Demarest said through the glass, smiling, of course.

"No-one's here but the boss."

"That is perfectly acceptable," Demarest said. "Please, open the door. Allow me entrance."

"Read it, numb-nuts" the guard said louder while pointing to a white sign on the door. The sign stated, in gold leafed lettering: *'After Hours - By appointment only'.*

The smile on Demarest's face changed from a grin to a grimace in a beat. His voice even regained some of its natural demonic tone.

"You are starting to become a hindrance to me, you vile insect."

The guard stood for a moment, sizing up this well-dressed visitor. He had a clear height advantage over the stranger. He also had a company issued firearm in his holster - in case anyone ever tried anything stupid. And he wasn't gonna put up with any more of this asshole's shit.

*Vile insect? What kind of insult was that?*

Walking over to the door, he unlocked it. Not to let the man in, but to let himself half-out.

Unbuttoning the strap on his handgun, the guard placed his hand on its grip and stood in the open doorway.

"Buddy. I don't want to be the one to ruin your day. You need to leave."

Without even a flicker of intimidation, Demarest spoke with equal force.

"Move out of my path."

"I don't think so, *vile insect*," he said, mimicking Demarest's voice as best he could.

The Djinn hated humans at the best of times, but none so much as when they lacked the respect his kind deserved.

The guard continued, "We ain't open to the public, how many ways I gotta say it—"

"Do you have any idea how frustrating it is to have unlimited power, but only be able to use it when some stupid worm asks you for something?"

"I don't give a single, solitary about you and your frustrations, pal," the guard said.

"Ask me for something. Ask me for *anything*! I offer this to you."

"You fucking dumb as well as deaf? I'm asking you to leave! Go!"

After a beat, Demarest's feet turned, leading him away. There was no twisting the guard's words. No stealing his life from him in a torrent of violence. The guard had asked him to leave. He had to leave. If there was no interpreting some vaguery in a wish, then there was nothing a Djinn could do to pervert and turn it back onto the wisher. This guard had spoken with frustrating simplicity, and his wish was granted.

As Demarest's feet carried him away, he pleaded, "I have to get inside! Allow me passage!"

At that, the guard fully stepped on the sidewalk, the glass door slowly closing behind him. "You want in, you'll have to go through me. And that's something I'd love to see."

Demarest's feet immediately stopped and the grin of malicious intent returned to his stolen face. Then he said, with joyful malice, "As you wish."

. . .

Walking through the foyer of the Auctioneer, Demarest smiled to himself as he left his newly created art piece by the entrance. A decoration for the glass frontage of the business; a fleshy painting in multiple hues of red. All smeared in an explosive pattern away from a steaming skeleton that lay slumped on the pavement. The flesh and blood looked like impasto on a canvas. Each morsel of meat spread in straight lines, with differing thicknesses, away from the body and up the glass in a circular pattern - like a crimson halo sprouting from the skeleton's skull.

As Demarest reached the security door at the rear of the foyer, he glanced back and noticed his shoes had left moist wet red footprints in their wake. Satisfied, he turned back, held up the guard's ID badge to the reader, and gained entrance to the offices of the Auctioneer.


In his office, Nick Merritt sat at his desk, atop which sat a few high-priced antiques - Personal favorites that he kept in here, held from sale for the moment so that he could appreciate them fully. He always felt that he gave these antiques far more reverence than those who bought them did.

His fingers hammered numbers into a calculator, and his other hand filled out a ledger with his antique fountain pen. As long as each entry he made was over his ten thousand dollar baseline, then he was a happy man. That was his bar for any antique worth his time. Of course the business had no choice but to deal with items that fell below this price, but they were things he would never involve himself personally with - and his staff knew this, so they kept those items out of his sight. Every time he had to write any of these lower prices down, he marked them with an asterisk. This mark carried with it no meaning other than to annoy him. So when he looked at the book, if he saw an abundance of these marks, he knew he was not doing his job properly. He wanted to cater to only the highest of the high class, and that asterisk was a flag to say *'Not there yet, Merritt'.* He hated that he had to have a storefront where *anyone* could just walk in - but at the end of the day, he suffered this annoyance in silence, keeping steadfast in his dream to one day switch to a more exclusive business model.

He suddenly became aware of his office door closing behind him. *That damned guard,* he thought; Merrit had specifically told him he didn't want any interruptions.

As he spun on his chair, Nick met the gaze of Nathaniel Demarest. Like all people obsessed with money and the acquisition of it, he was aware of the danger of other people's greed. Maybe this well-dressed man was a well-dressed thief? Maybe he broke in and did not expect to find anyone in these offices? Immediately, Nick rolled his chair to the side, to block the view of the valuable items that sat on his desk; a gesture Demarest registered with an amused smirk.

"Who the hell are you?" Nick demanded. "How the hell did you get in here?"

"The guard. He..." Demarest stopped, smirked, then continued. "He opened up for me."

Before Nick could voice any further objections, Demarest continued.

"I am looking for Alexandra Amberson. You may be able to assist me in finding her address?"

*Okay*, Nick thought, very relieved. *Not a thief.*

"She didn't come in. She was sick today. May I ask who you are? Why do you want her address?" Nick asked. He relaxed a bit more, no longer concerned for his antiques.

"I am somebody she is expecting," Demarest said.

"If she knows you, then why don't you already know where she lives?"

Nick leaned back into his chair, placed his hands behind his head, and attempted a power play on this stranger; exuding relaxation to throw the stranger off-guard.

"Our dealings with each other have not been in the flesh. Now, please—"

"Met online, did you?" Nick said.

"Something like that."

Demarest weighed up the man in front of him.

"Then you best drop her an email. I will not give out staff details to any old person who asks. You understand that, right? You could be anyone. You could be a stalker for all I know, and I will not put my staff in danger."

"I understand perfectly," Demarest said, wondering what this man's demise would taste like. "Would you know where she is right now?"

"I would, but as I said, since you seem to not be listening, I will not tell you."

Without an argument, Demarest turned to a plinth standing beside him. Upon it sat a Ballet Russe dancer in marble, bronze, and jade. Gingerly, he picked up the classic art déco statuette.

"Hey!" Nick said as he looked at this visitor with a rising contempt. *The nerve of this guy!*

"Exquisite, isn't it?" Demarest said, almost whispering. "Practically untouched by the ravages of time, unlike so many others of its kind.

"And extremely valuable. Now put it down."

Placing it back onto its plinth, Demarest asked, "Would you like it to become twice as valuable? Three times? Four?"

"I wish!" Nick replied with a surprised laugh. "Market is a bit quiet lately."

"As you wish."

Nick's attention turned to the statuette. Gone were the lesser metals, and the whole piece had been replaced with pure, solid gold.

Standing up from his desk, Nick strode over - past the visitor - and picked up the statuette. He ran his fingers over it in amazement.

"How... H-how did you?" he said, his eyes wide.

"An old family secret," Demarest said. "Now where is Alexandra?"

Nick's eyes didn't break from the statue as he replied, "I don't feel comfortable giving you that information. I've been telling you that repeatedly."

"Normally I only allow one wish, but I shall make an exception for you. You should feel honored about this. So tell me, what would make you feel comfortable to tell me? Just name your wish."

Nick had no idea of the reality of his situation. He only knew that he had just witnessed a man turn a statue from expensive, to priceless, without breaking a sweat. What else could he do?

"What's the limit?" Nick asked without thinking.

"The limit is your imagination. Just ask. What can I give you, in order for you to give me what I need to know?"

"I'm not greedy," Nick said.

"Of course not."

"Maybe a million dollars?"

Demarest smiled.

"As you wish..."

. . .

Within the departure terminal of a busy Texas airport, Tannoy speakers blared out their various announcements. Passengers scurried about with their carry-on luggage gripped tightly as they searched to find their gates.

At a booking counter, an elderly woman was purchasing her ticket.

"That will be eighty-nine dollars, please," the clerk in an overly happy and upbeat tone, and followed quickly with, "Can I also interest you in our flight insurance? Only another eleven dollars, making it a round one hundred, for your peace of mind."

Flustered and not wishing to appear rude, the elderly customer just nodded and handed over her credit card.

Taking the card, the clerk glanced back to her counter and took hold of a blank form from a tray.

"We just need the name of your next of kin." Handing over the form, she continued with a smile, "The beneficiary for any insurance claimed."

"Oh, of course," the elderly lady said. "That would be my son. Nicholas."

After scribbling in the details on the form, she handed it back to the clerk with a smile.

"And that is it. You are all good to go, Mrs. Merritt." the clerk said. Handing over a ticket to the elderly lady, she smiled in her best customer service way. "That is your ticket, please go up the escalator to Gate 22. And please enjoy your flight."


In the sky, somewhere over America, Flight 1919 disappeared from radars at 8:13 p.m. For those who happened to look up at that moment, they may have seen a momentary bright flash, as flames ripped through the passenger craft, sending its burning remains plummeting to the mountains below.

There were no survivors.

Eleanor Merritt's life insurance was worth one million dollars.

CHAPTER
# SIXTEEN

On the court, Alex's girls were now in two teams. Half were wearing red shirts and half wearing blue shirts; ready for a practice game between them for the benefit of the parents - who now sat on the benches of the court, either cheering, or carrying the vacant stare of someone who'd had to endure these types of things one too many times.

On the red team, Sierra ran, keeping control of the ball despite the blue-shirts' best efforts.

On the front bench, Alex sat in a daze, deep in thought; her mind not on the game in the slightest.

Meanwhile, Sierra made a run for the basket. Blue shirts approached from all directions to stop her.

Shannon, sitting next to Alex, nudged her. "Hey, *I'm* paying more attention than you, and I'm only your damn driver!"

Snapping out of it, Alex said, "I told you, you can go home."

Shaking her head, Shannon said, "I'm not coming back

out again to pick you up." She motioned to her watch. "Maybe half-time now? You're running those poor girls ragged."

Alex glanced at the game, and quickly put the whistle to her mouth, but before she blew into it, her eyes landed on Sierra, who avoided an attempted tackle, spun on the spot, jumped, and then threw. It was just like Alex had taught her during their last lesson - with the ball rebounding off the backboard, then falling defiantly through the hoop. A smile crept over Alex's face as the game temporarily pushed her worries aside.

Alex blew the whistle, bringing the game to a temporary halt.

"Half-time ladies. Take ten," Alex said.

As the red team ran around their star player, they took turns giving her high-fives. Mid-celebration, Sierra beamed over toward Alex with pride. "Stillness, Ms. Amberson! *Stillness*, just like you said!"

Alex nodded, happy. Then as soon as Sierra and her winning team ran off to join the blue-shirts at the refreshment table, Alex's worry returned, and she turned to Shannon.

"Can I borrow your phone?" Alex asked.

"Again?" Shannon said, exasperated. "You're supposed to be running a game for these girls, not calling a teacher about goddamn fairy tales."

Alex wished she hadn't told Shannon anything about any of this. Though, of course she had kept the parts about the Djinn out of it. She didn't want Shannon doubting her sanity as much as she doubted it herself.

Holding the phone out, Shannon said, "Why can't you just use the pay phone over there?"

"I haven't got any change for that," Alex said, as she took

the phone. She then hit the *redial* button and turned her attention to the call.

It rang and rang, then cut to the answering machine.

"Shit," Alex said. As the message ended, and the familiar beep was heard, Alex spoke into the phone. "Professor Derleth? Hi, this is Alex. Again. I really need to talk to you. Can you call me back please? Thanks."

Alex hung up and offered the phone back to Shannon, who looked at her blankly.

Alex, noticing that Shannon wasn't taking the phone from her, said, "What is it?"

With a sigh, Shannon said, "Well, no point me taking it, is there? When you're giving out my number to people to call you back!"

"Oh." Alex didn't even realize what she had done. "Well, you can hold it for a moment, can't you? I gotta go speak to the girls."

"Driver and receptionist. Great!"

Shannon took the phone. Alex smiled sheepishly then hurried over to where the girls gathered. Forcing herself to focus on the task at hand, she plastered on a big smile.

"Great game, girls!"


Shannon sighed as she watched her sister across the court.

"Excuse me, miss?"

Turning in her seat, Shannon saw a well-dressed man holding out a twenty-dollar bill toward her.

"I couldn't help but notice you have a phone. Would it be a terrible imposition if I could make a quick call on it? I can, of course, pay you."

Shannon looked at him with a smile. Nice. Polite. Handsome. Willing to pay over the odds. A rarity.

"Seems my phone's a free-for-all today, so no harm in you joining in the fun."

She handed him the phone and waved away the proffered cash.

"That is very kind of you," the man said as he took the phone from her hand.

Smiling, Shannon turned back around in her seat, then started to daydream what this man may ask her next, and what else she might give to him for free.

What Shannon couldn't see was that the finely-dressed man had hit the *redial* button, mimicking what Alex had done before. He had paid attention; watched Alex from his seat behind her. Alex had been unaware of his presence. She had not even felt it when he grazed her hair. When he marked her to him. She could not run away now. She could not hide. He had found her.

Shannon waited as the man secretly listened to the outgoing message at the other end of the phone. "Hello, this is Professor Wendy Derleth. Please leave a message after the tone."

*Beep.*

Hanging up the call, Demarest mouthed the name *Wendy Derleth*, committing it to memory.

Tapping Shannon on the shoulder, he handed her the phone back with a smile.

"Most kind of you. These are useful little contraptions, aren't they?"

He got up from his bench seat and made his way toward the exit.

*Shame*, Shannon thought. *Could have been fun.*

As she watched him walk away, she pondered his weird turn of phrase; useful contraptions? How old *was* he? Where had *he* been the past few years?

. . .

Across the court, Alex was busy lacing up one of her players' shoes.

"There, that should keep you from...tripping..."

Her words trailed off. She sensed something nearby. A presence. The feeling of being watched. A feeling of something horrible. A primal fear.

The hairs on the back of her neck stood up. A chill spilled down her spine. She looked up and around her.

The parents in the aisles looked happy; her sister looked annoyed as she seemingly did with more frequency nowadays; the kids all talked happily amongst themselves, all waiting for the start of the second half of the game.

Her eyes shifted focus beyond the girls, beyond the parents, to the end of the benches that were in front of the exit.

Ale's eyes widened as she met the gaze of a man - the face she saw in her visions. The false face that covered the monster's true face. There was no mistaking him.

The evil was indeed very real.

He had let her sense him in that moment. He smiled hungrily as a group of five girls ran across Alex's field of vision.

When they passed...

...Demarest was gone.

# YOUR SECOND WISH

There are no longer any illusions.

Gone are my veils.

You had sought to peek beyond the curtain of reality.

Now you have learned what I am, what I offer, what I am capable of.

Of course, you may wish to walk away now.

You may wish for no more.

You may wish for escape.

You may abandon these writings, guided by your own free will.

But then, my tale would remain half-told.

Yet you have only made one wish. Why not use another to know the truth? To learn how this tale inevitably ends?

One more wish could not hurt, could it?

You are still here? You desire more?

*As you wish....*

# A Dark Wonderland

# CHAPTER
# SEVENTEEN

The wind picked up, as night fully enveloped the city. The dark pendulous clouds above started to gently release their moisture, until it soon became a heavy torrential downpour, soaking the city.

On a residential street, in the alleys and crevices where the light did not reach, the shadows seemed to undulate in a rhythmic heartbeat, signaling the arrival of the Djinn, unperturbed by the rain. As if something was sitting in the dark; breathing, waiting. Just out of reach of this reality, yet existing at the precipice, patiently.

With his suit getting darker as each raindrop soaked into the material, Demarest stood on the sidewalk, focused, as he stared up at the expensive apartment building in front of him. The glow from the streetlamp beside him appeared to dim in his presence, as if in fear of fully casting him in any of their brightness. The grin never left his face as he walked up the rain-slicked steps and entered the dry foyer to the building.

. . .

This night soon gave way to the rising sun. It was morning now.The storm had passed, taking with it the rainfall which had briefly cleansed the city. It's only legacy; the dissipating puddles that decorated the streets and sidewalks.

High up in the expensive apartment building, within one tastefully furnished apartment, the sunlight-filled living room had a comforting brilliance. The two white sofas seemed spectacularly brighter than they should have been, as the thin white curtains blocked nothing, only distorting the view, the light permeating through them with ease.

A door to the adjacent bedroom opened, and Demarest walked out, and into the center of the room. He sat at the smaller of the two sofas.

He looked around - casting appraising glances - judging the decor and the possessions of the person who had once dwelled here.

A sly smile crawled up his lips. His plan was proceeding exactly as it should.

He leaned forward and pulled the coffee table nearer to him. Putting one hand in his pocket, he pulled out the four pieces of the fractured opal.

As he held these pieces in his hand, a change started to occur within them; these cursed pieces stripped away all the bodily illusion he had created with his dark magic. The hair on his head dissipated like burning embers, lifting off like particles in the wind from his leathery scalp, then floated into nothingness on an imaginary breeze. The face he had stolen slipped off of his own, like a fleshy, greasy mass, crawling down a windowpane. The mask fell from his face. He caught it in his hand, and placed it on the coffee table. Droplets of blood trailed the Djinn's face. It was no longer the man called Nathaniel Demarest - though it still wore his fine suit. It was now a demon in human clothing.

As if sympathetic to the dark nature of this being, the sunlight shrank away, leaving the room in dark shadow.

In the recesses of the supernaturally emboldened darkness, hidden, wicked things moved ever so slightly. Movements that suggested terrible anatomies writhing beneath their inscrutable blackness. From somewhere within, the whispers that followed him could be heard again. Terrible mutterings from the most despicable creatures.

Closing its clawed hand, the Djinn held the pieces of the opal tightly. As it concentrated, a glowing red emanated from between its claws.

"I claim that which is owed," it said.

No trace of its human voice remained.


In her apartment, Alex's phone rang. She picked it up.

"Ms. Amberson?" said the voice on the other end.

Alex recognized it, but still asked out of habit, "Yes, it is; who is this?"

"It's Detective Nathanson. Do you have a moment to talk?

Alex actually smiled. She did not know why, but Nathanson had a calming demeanor. He may have been young, but he was there for her in a big way when she had found out about Josh. Any other detective would have thrown her out of the lab, or arrested her as a suspect.

"Of course, Detective. How can I help?

"A guy was in here asking about you. I meant to call you before, but we had a bit of an emergency. He-" Suddenly cutting himself off mid-sentence, his voice became strangled. The words trailed off as he strained to speak.

Simultaneously, Alex dropped the phone as her legs gave way, collapsing on the floor. It was happening again. Her mind filled with a new red-tinted hell-vision. But this one was occurring right now, and she saw Nathanson's eyes rolling up into their sockets in a ghastly version of the police station. She witnessed him gasp for a second, then drop to the floor in a seizure.

Unable to see anything in her own world, Alex scrambled, blindly, as best she could in order to recover the phone receiver; the one Nathanson had been at the other end of.

Finding it dangling from the kitchen counter, she screamed in a panic, "Hello?! Detective, are you okay?" As if what she witnessed may still be a lie. She pleaded for a reply, but simultaneously could see him shaking on the floor, beginning to froth at the mouth. The shouts of the men were around him in her vision, and were repeated a fraction of a second later over the phone.

Then her vision blurred beyond definition and shifted. Now she was not with the detective anymore, but in a makeshift homeless encampment underneath a railway overpass. The homeless man who had wished death on the pharmacist a couple of nights ago, now sat on the disused porch of a nearby building, playing cards with two others. Playing with cigarettes as currency.

"I raise you two smokes," one of the other men said.

Before he could reply, the homeless man tensed, as if being hit with thousands of volts of electricity. His eyes bugged out and his teeth bit into his tongue. As he screamed, blood poured out between his teeth and into his yellowing beard.

Alex, still locked into the vision, scrambled to stand; trying to overcome the debilitating pain these episodes wrought. She dropped the receiver and reached out to find anything she could lift herself up with.

The vision blurred, and then shifted again, this time focusing inside the day room of a psychiatric hospital. The med-student who had walked in on the Djinn stealing the corpse's face was now a patient here; broken by his experience. Eyes wrapped in bandages. Alex watched as the hospital porters tried their best to subdue him on the floor. The student loosed a blood-curdling wail as he brutally slammed his head over and over onto the stone tile, his skull splitting on impact. The hospital porters were unable to stop him, because of how violently he thrashed.

What they didn't know was that the pain in his head had built to such an intensity, he would do anything to make it stop.

With her body convulsing in shock, Alex fell back onto the edge of her coffee table as the corner of her eyes slowly started to weep bloody tears.

Yet again her vision brought her to another place; a dimly lit storeroom where a collection of mannequins stood at one end. The mannequin that was once a beautiful young woman named Ariella cried in mute silence, and the plastic she was made of cracked, causing blood to seep out from within.

All but unconscious, Alex lay slack-jawed and drooling on her apartment floor.

As this vision faded, she prayed to any God that would listen for a respite.

None answered her.

The vision stole her away yet again, this time granting her a view of the office of Nick Merritt. The man replaced the handset of the phone on his desk, his cheeks slicked with tears that fell uncontrollably.

"Mommy," he sobbed. "No."

Just as he lowered his head into his hands, his body - like the others - was suddenly hit with an insurmountable psychic violence. He screamed as his veins popped to the surfaces of his neck and temples.

"Help me!"

His voice echoed throughout the building.

Two rooms away, in the foyer, Shannon heard her employer's screams.

As she ran out from the foyer, she did not notice the bloodied footprints left by the Djinn the previous night. Nor did she see the remnants of the guard that had been smashed into pulp at the front entrance. The coating of his blood that had slicked the glass frontage had been washed away by the heavy rain.

Back in his new apartment, the Djinn sat in the shadowed living room. He still held onto the shards of the opal, and they continued to glow in his clenched fist. Brighter and brighter the glow pulsed. With each wave of light, the shadows beat at the same rhythm. So too, did the Djinn's own body - as if all were conjoined in a diabolical dance - to a crescendo as the Djinn opened its clawed hand, revealing the opal now sat there, impossibly in one piece again - sitting in magnificence in its palm; the magic it controlled on full display.

As it glanced down at the gem with its glistening dark eyes, the usual whispers from the shadows started to rise and become more raucous. Growls and snarls deep from within another reality grew in ferocity.

"Patience," the Djinn snarled.

Grabbing the stolen face off the coffee table, the Djinn held it up to his own with one hand, and with the other closed his hand over the opal once more.

For a brief second, the room sank into an unimaginable blackness, before returning a moment later.

The Djinn was gone; Nathaniel Demarest returned in its

place. The sun cascaded once more through the thin white curtains.

Staring at the opal, Demarest held it up to his eye and smiled.

"Complete the inevitable, Alexandra. Three wishes are yours to claim."


Alex lay, unconscious, on the floor of her apartment, for over an hour. The visions had drained her energy.

It was only when Shannon walked through the front door in tears that Alex began to stir.

"Alex No!" Shannon screamed and rushed over to Alex.

As Shannon helped her to her feet, Alex looked around groggily, attempting to keep her focus.

"What happened?" Shannon asked, her voice sheer terror.

"I don't know..." Alex said, slowly.


After moving Alex to a chair, and Alex's repeated insistence that she was ok, Shannon told her about Nick's collapse and his admittance to hospital.

"Is he okay?" Alex asked weakly.

"Not really. They had to isolate him."

Trying to collect her thoughts as best she could, Alex asked, "Did Professor Derleth return my call?"

"Jesus, Alex. What's wrong with you lately? We've got a sick friend. You keep passing out. Don't you even care? You're so focused o -"

"It's all connected," Alex said, interrupting. "Please. Did she call back?"

"Yeah, actually. She said she wants you to go to her place.

She left her address." Reaching into her pocket, Shannon brought out a piece of paper. "Here. Take it."

Re-prioritizing things in her mind, Alex took the paper, but then looked at her sister. "Can we go see Nick?"

Shannon's reply was all sarcasm. "You don't wanna bail again and see this woman, instead?"

"No, let's go see Nick." Alex didn't rise to the bait. She was too exhausted. "I'll see Professor Derleth later."

CHAPTER

# EIGHTEEN

In the isolation ward of the city hospital, accompanied by a clipboard-carrying doctor, Alex and Shannon walked along a lengthy hallway. The doctor slowed when they got to a large glass window, which looked into a ward containing three beds.

Further along the glass walls, two policemen stood looking in at one of the beds.

In that bed, Nick lay unconscious. Wired to monitoring machines, oxygen and an IV drip, he - along with the other two patients - was isolated within an individually sealed plastic environment. Attending nurses, dressed in their own protective hazardous material suits, were with each patient. It seemed all three patients had suffered the same infirmity.

"My God." Alex's eyes widened in shock as she saw the extent of Nick's condition. Turning to the doctor, she asked, "Why the suits? What's happened?"

Alex's mind spun in confusion. If her visions were true, she'd seen Nick collapse with no visible cause.

"Strict isolation is protocol, I'm afraid," the doctor said, flatly. "Three similar cases with no obvious cause, we have to follow CDC guidelines."

"So you don't know what's wrong?" Shannon said.

The doctor shook his head. "I hate to say it, but no. We honestly have no idea. We've never seen anything like this before. So, we can't rule anything out."

Alex, listening, scanned the ward on the other side of the glass. As a nurse at the bed to the left moved out of the way, Alex realized that Nick was not the only person she knew in this room. Another person she'd seen in her vision lay in that bed; The man she had been on the phone with.

"Nathanson," Alex muttered under her breath, now understanding the presence of the police officers a few feet away.

Shannon turned to Alex, surprised. "What?"

The two policemen turned to look at her as well, some signs of recognition dancing across their faces. Alex started to panic about the possibility of being seen here. Had either of them been at Josh's lab? Could they think she was the cause of this? be the cause of this.

"You know him?" the doctor said.

"Barely, I met him last week," Alex said, looking at the policemen in her periphery. "Is he suffering from the same thing as Nick?" she asked, hoping to be told it was unrelated, to disprove her visions. Never before in her life had she wanted to be the crazy one. Not until these visions had begun plaguing her. The alternative was too terrifying to comprehend.

"I am afraid so," the doctor said. "Comatose. Eyes open. Low life signs, minimal brain activity."

"His eyes look blank," Shannon said, on the verge of tears. "Like they have nothing inside them."

She'd never really liked Nick, but she would never have wished this kind of pain on anyone.

"What about the other one?" Alex asked, looking to the bed on the right. "Is there a homeless guy, or a young man without eyes in that last bed?"

The doctor looked at her, thoroughly confused.

Alex remembered a line of text from her research:

*...The Stone of the Secret Fire was said to be powered by the human soul. The king's sorcerer sacrificed dozens of condemned prisoners to enable the stone to contain enough strength to imprison the Djinn within its walls...*

"No," Alex said weakly, as she continued to stare into the room. She stepped forward and placed her palm on the glass.

As her skin hit the glass, she was pulled away yet again from this reality and thrown into another vision. Unlike the others, this one was not in any place she could determine.

She stood in a large, shadowed chamber with a concave roof which bellied down in curved walls to meet the floor. This was a terrible place where the large supporting struts resembled ribs, as they curved up each side of the room. Like red hot metal, they radiated up the walls to the center of the domed ceiling high above. Whatever this place was, Alex was alone here - as far as she could initially determine.

Before she could take in the totality of this room, screams filled the air, and her vision became flooded with multiple terrifying images of pain and torture. Tentacles. Cuts. Blood. Twisting. Breaking. Burning. Each flash was indistinguishable yet unmistakably grotesque. Nightmarish glimpses into the vilest reaches of evil.

The images ceased, as quickly as they had begun, leaving her back in the large chamber. But now - she was no longer alone.

At the end of the room opposite her, there was now a throne, made from freshly severed body parts. And upon this throne sat Nathaniel Demarest. Finely suited and looking very out of place. Only his devilish grin and devious eyes looked like they belonged here.

He stood and took a step toward her, his eyes locking onto hers.

"Only *you* can end their suffering, Alexandra. Only *you* can free them."

Alex screamed. She saw that she was being held by both Shannon and the doctor.

"Alex!" Shannon said.

Bursting free from her vision, Alex scrambled out of their arms and across to the other side of the corridor. The policemen still regarded her strangely and, in her panic - Alex thought - accusingly.

The doctor approached her slowly, "Ms. Amberson, how-"

"Leave me alone!" she said, then held her hands out to keep the doctor at bay. "I'm okay."

But, she did not sound or look okay. She was practically hyperventilating. It was all finally getting to be too much for her.

By her estimation, the two policemen seemed as if they had certainly made a connection between her and their fallen comrade. They glanced back toward their friend in the ward and talked in hushed tones. But before they could look back, Alex had gotten to her feet and rushed away, as fast as she could run - leaving the doctor and Shannon staring after her in shock.

Slamming the door shut behind her, Alex sat in the driver's seat of her car.

Her breathing was out of control, and tears tumbled down her cheeks.

Looking around in a panic, she saw the hospital parking lot was devoid of any life. She could only see the rows and rows of empty cars parked all around her.

Catching a glimpse of herself in the rear-view mirror, she paused. She hardly recognized this fragile, pale, frightened, and all-too-human girl staring back at her. The strong woman she always tried to be was gone. Her nerves were raw; she sobbed harder.

Her mind swirled with the memories of the awful visions. All those people convulsing in the supernatural grip of a diabolical presence. Nick and Nathanson lying in comas from the injuries she had impossibly seen. What of the others? That guy in the psych ward? The vagrant playing cards? The bleeding mannequin? As her mind turned these events over and over again, all she could hear was the voice. *That* voice.

*Only you can free them.*

She closed her eyes and took a deep breath. There had to be a different explanation. Something that made the slightest bit of sense.

This couldn't be a fucking *genie*!

Opening her eyes again, she tried to regain her composure, but the tears continued.

"I can't do this," she whispered under her breath. "I just can't."

Trying again to snap herself out of her thoughts, she shook her head.

Reaching over to the passenger side, she opened her glove box. A bottle of pills rolled into view, nestled amongst the various vehicle-related papers.

She grabbed the bottle, unscrewed the lid, and shook a pill into her hand. Maybe she needed them after all. *Maybe Shannon was right*, she thought.

As if on cue, the passenger-side door opened, and Shannon got in, the anger on her face dissipating when she saw the distraught condition Alex was in. Concern overtook any frustration she had felt.

"Alex?" Shannon's voice was unusually soft.

With her lip quivering, and a pill in her hand, Alex turned to her sister, showing bloodshot eyes. "Should I?" Alex asked with a broken voice, motioning to the pill. "It's me... isn't it?"

"You'll be okay," Shannon reassured her. "Just take it. It'll all be fine. I'm here for you. Like last time. You'll be you again."

About to take the pill, she forced a weak smile. "Please tell me it's all just a coincidence."

"You know you asked who the other guy was? A tramp or a guy without eyes?"

"Yeah." Alex said, smiling. With a glimmer of hope that her nightmare visions had failed to come true, and could be fixed if she just took the pill, she sighed in relief.

"The Doctor said it was a woman, someone had stuck her inside of a mannequin somehow. Molded her in. It was the seizure that broke her free from it. No one-"

"What?" Alex lowered the pill.

"What's wrong?" Shannon asked.

"I saw them...I saw them *all*!"

"What the hell are you talking about? Just take the goddamn pill, Alex."

Shannon's concern abated as she saw that her sister was losing her grip on reality, just as she had after the fire.

Throwing the pill to the footwell beneath her, Alex slammed the steering wheel.

"No!" she said. "It isn't me! None of this!"

"You're scaring me," Shannon said, afraid.

"If it's a fight he wants, then he's gonna fucking get one."

"Who? What are you talking about?"

"The fucking Djinn," Alex screamed in anger. "Fuck him! How fucking *dare he*!"

# NINETEEN

"Alexandra, sorry for all the telephone tennis. I am not very good with phones." Wendy Derleth said as she held the door open wide to her apartment, beckoning Alex in with her other hand.

With a nod of thanks, Alex walked in. Though her tears had gone, her demeanor exuded the weariness of a traumatic week.

Wendy continued, "I believe in face to face. Anything else..." She shut the door behind Alex. "Well let's just say I have to see it to believe it."

"Isn't that counterproductive for someone teaching folklore?" Alex replied.

"You know? I never thought of that correlation before, Alexandra."

"Please, call me Alex."

"Of course." Wendy motioned Alex into the living room.

Alex glanced around at the decor of the professor's home. It was bright, well-kept, with long flowing white curtains. Though she didn't know it, this was the apartment where Demarest had recently sat and reconfigured the opal.

"I just came from the hospital," Alex said.

"Oh, dear." Wendy turned to Alex, a surprised look on her face. "Nothing wrong, I hope?"

"I really don't know how to say this..."

Wendy motioned to the sofa. "Please, sit."

Nodding, Alex sat in the middle on a large three-seater sofa, as Wendy sat on the sofa opposite. The same place where the Djinn, disguised as Demarest, had sat before.

"Now what's so difficult?" Wendy said.

"The opal. The Stone of the Secret Fire?"

"Yes? What about it?"

"It's been charged."

Wendy's smile faltered. "What do you mean? Charged?"

"I read it in those books you recommended. It needs to be charged with souls to have power. Like the sorcerer did when he trapped the Djinn. He-"

"I'm sorry, Alex," Wendy said. "I'm lost."

"It's been charged again. He has taken at least five souls." Alex said each word carefully, pleading to be believed. "I saw them all."

"It's the twentieth century, Alex," said Wendy, as she sat back in her seat. "Don't you think that sounds a bit unlikely? These stories are all parables, not facts."

Alex waved her hand dismissively. "I don't care how it sounds, please... just hear me out. Something terrible is going on. I thought you of all people would understand. You know about all of this!"

Considering her words, Wendy said, "I suppose I *should*. But Alex, really-"

"Listen." Alex sat forward. "Let's say I'm crazy. That's fine. Let's say this is all hypothetical. Okay? Is that better?"

Wendy nodded, slightly amused. "Okay then, what do you mean? Hypothetically?"

"Let's just say - as I said, hypothetically - that somehow, some way, the Djinn were real."

Wendy nodded again. "Let us say that."

"And let us say, somehow I woke a Djinn from being trapped within the Stone of the Secret Fire."

"So, you are saying that the opal you mentioned before, was the *actual* fabled gem. The one whose existence was never corroborated, but only written about in one obscure text?"

"Yes." Alex said. "Now let's also say, somehow - some way - this Djinn that had been awakened, was loose."

"Loose?"

"Collecting souls. Granting wishes. Doing exactly what it got a necromancer to allow it to do before. It's not restrained by God's curse. It found a way around that to grant wishes to anyone, so it could get more and more power. Just like with the Persian king."

"This is a lot to suppose."

"It's all hypothetical, though," Alex reminded her. "Now let us *finally* say that the Djinn has found souls to charge this stone. He would have a lot of power now. So, he would be ready to finish things off by forcing *me* - his liberator - to make three wishes. Then he can use the stone to bring his kind back from the void, instead of someone sending him back there."

Wendy paused for a moment and regarded Alex.

"What makes you think the stone can do that? What makes you believe that a stone with the same power that held this Djinn can do something like break a hole through reality, enough to bring a whole race of monsters through?"

"Logic."

"None of this sounds remotely logical."

"Well, why else would the Djinn charge the stone with

souls? He wouldn't want to be trapped again, so the stone's power must therefore be used for something else. It stands to reason that this power is what he will use. So, what I am asking is: what do I do? How can I fight him?"

"Well now," Wendy said with a smirk, "I would say, and please forgive the vernacular, that you are fucked."

Alex didn't know how to reply to this.

"Alex, indulge me. I'll play devil's advocate."

"Okay." Alex felt that Wendy was not close to remotely believing her, but she was grateful to have her hypothesis indulged.

"What did the Djinn use to collect this 'powerful charge' with the Persian King if the stone was not his yet?"

Alex was immediately at a loss.

"You mention logic. *That* is a gap in the logic, isn't it? And secondly, why do you keep referring to the Djinn as a 'he'?"

"I... Well that doesn't really matter does it?" Alex felt they were straying from the point of the conversation.

"Well, this is *your* hypothetical, and within it there are gaps in logic and presumption. Saying 'Oh the stone is charged and will end the world' or whatever, is a big leap. Especially as none of the texts mention the stone as this kind of weapon. Not one. It was a container. So you are appropriating your own mythology to the story."

"But-"

"Let me finish," Wendy said. "And you may feel that presuming the Djinn to be male is just a harmless thought, but in logical discourse, *any* presumption is a slippery slope. Do you understand?"

Alex did. Spelled out like that, she started to doubt her convictions. She was presuming a lot, making guesses without facts. Just piecing bits together, using her feelings.

"I do understand." Alex's voice grew soft, and she became lost in thought.

Alex's defenses lowered, and she somehow felt herself doubting her own sanity once more. All the while, mere feet away, Wendy Derleth's bedroom door was ajar. And just beyond that door, a naked body lay on the four-poster bed within. The sun shone in through the window, illuminating everything it touched. Bathed in this sunlight, a dead woman lay marinating in her own crimson essence. This body's face was missing, having been cut clean off - in exactly the same way as the cadaver the Djinn had found in the anatomy room. But this fresh corpse also lied in a mass of gouges and ripped flesh, more closely resembling the victim of a terribly vicious animal attack than a cold-blooded murder. These desecrated remains were all that was left of the body of Professor Wendy Derleth.

"Would you like something to drink, by the way?" the thing calling itself Wendy Derleth asked as it stood up from the sofa.

Alex shook her head and replied with a polite smile. "No, I'm fine. Thank you."

"Really? Well, I think I shall indulge myself," Wendy replied as she looked around the room.

Alex thought, for a second, that it seemed her host did not know where she kept the drinks in her own apartment. But before Alex could consider this anymore, Wendy strode over to an antique cabinet at the far side of the room, which housed some bottles of liquor.

Wendy poured herself a stiff scotch and motioned to the cabinet. "Your employer would like this, wouldn't he? Nice antique, could fetch a decent price."

Alex was taken aback. "My boss? I don't remember telling you who I worked for."

Wendy laughed. "You didn't? I'm not sure how I would know, then." She took a swig of her drink and walked back over to the sofa.

Something suddenly clicked for Alex. "Maybe Beaumont mentioned it? Sorry, I didn't mean to be defensive."

"Beaumont! Yes, that's it."

Sitting back on the sofa, Wendy placed what was left of her drink on the coffee table in front of her. "Now back to the matter at hand. Your hypothetical. You're obviously hoping for some spell, some piece of magic, that would have been written in one of the texts. Something that would enable you to vanquish said Djinn. Correct?"

"Yes."

"Well, then certainly one must have existed. Not that one can kill it, of course, as you can't kill what is never born. But to contain it, like the sorcerer did in Persia." Wendy took the last swig of her drink and returned the now-empty glass to the table. "But those spells and incantations were only in the minds of those long-since-dead. Not everyone had a grasp on magic." Changing the subject, she continued, "Would you like me to put the heating on? You look a bit cold."

Wendy's over-attentiveness was starting to grate on Alex, but she didn't want to show it. Wendy was gracious enough just to be talking to her, after all.

"No, no I'm fine," Alex said, barely masking her curtness.

"You are sure? Nothing I can do for you at the moment?"

Bordering on rudeness, Alex shot back, "No."

"Well I am sure there is *something* I can do," said Wendy, ignoring Alex's growing impatience.

"Wendy, please!" Alex implored. "Just talk to me."

"Okay, dear. Where was I? Oh yes. Spells. Sorcerers. You were born into an Age of Reason, Alex. An Age of Science. Whatever was not written down didn't survive across the ages, at least not in any books I have heard of. All that remains are some vague references to some unknown magic or power. No other details. Certainly no spells that have any substance beyond superstition."

Wendy stopped there and smiled slightly, clearly enjoying the conversation.

Alex said, "But the Djinn himself-"

"*ITself*, Alex." Wendy corrected.

"Yes, sorry." Alex was getting flustered.

"The *hypothetical* Djinn."

"But the existence of the Djinn would prove that magic at least exists somehow. That it is real. Which would mean the world cannot be *just* reason and science. There is magic too, right? It must be *somewhere*!" Alex felt herself clutching at straws. Alex understood what Wendy was saying, but she also knew what she had witnessed. What that *thing* had said to her. Wendy might say it was not a man, but what she saw in that red chamber was. She was *sure* of it.

Wendy eyed her empty glass, pondering another as she replied, "The Djinn, *should* they exist, would be *all there was*. Imagine that. The only magical thing in a rational world. A defenseless world of disbelievers. Where all the reason in the world could not save you, nor could science rescue you. You do realize what you are saying, hypothetically, right?"

Alex did not reply.

"*If* the Djinn exist. Then it would not just be you that was in danger, but the entire world. The Djinn would have a fine old time here." Wendy chuckled. "Decimating the world in a glorious fashion!"

"This isn't a joke!" Alex said.

"Of course it isn't. It is hypothetical, as we've agreed." Wendy fell silent. Alex started to look anxious. "Can I get you something to eat? I am a wizard in the kitchen, and it is way past my lunch time."

Losing control, Alex stood and said in a raised voice, "Wendy, please. I am not hungry. I am not thirsty. I am not cold. Why are you constantly asking me what I want? What I-"

Suddenly her voice cut off.

Her mind reeled; a frozen second where the weight of the thought she now considered was almost crushing her.

"Alex?" Wendy said, a wry smile still on her face.

"I'm sorry." Alex said, forcing a happier demeanor, swallowing her fear down. "I'm a little tense. It's been... a hard week."

"You seem quite angry at me." The smile still did not fade. "Are you?"

"No, it's not you. Honestly, I'm okay. I..." Her mind screamed at her to keep her cool. "I just need rest, I think."

"Alright, so where were we again?" Wendy spoke. Alex sat back down. "No spells. No hope. Hypothetically."

"There is always hope." Alex said, to herself more than to Wendy; Steeling her determination.

"You think so?" Wendy said, clearly enjoying this conversation more and more, despite, or maybe because of, Alex's ever-increasing hysteria.

"If there is no magic, then the hope rests on me," Alex said.

"So, against a hypothetical being with magic unknown by the modern age, you, Alexandra Amberson, will rely on *yourself* to vanquish ancient and unknowable evil?"

"Right."

"And you will rely on what? Your courage? Your nerve? Your wits?"

Alex nodded.

"You will take these things of yours, and face an eternal being."

"Right," Alex repeated.

"March right up, and match wits with a creature older than the human race. Battle with the Prince of the Dark Dominion?" Wendy's smile was slipping. Getting more serious by the word. Alex's presumption seemed to have rankled her. "Pit your tiny twentieth century mind against one who has dwelt in the void between the worlds? Stand up against something that has trod on the wings of angels?"

Alex watched Wendy's facade slowly drop, and her inner terror was matched only by her forced stoicism.

Wendy suddenly smiled again, the mask once more replaced at speed. "Oh Alex, you are a delight. You truly are."

"I am glad I can amuse you," Alex said.

"Have I offended you?" Wendy leaned forward. "I'm sorry, let me make it up to you. What can I offer-"

"No, that's okay," Alex interrupted. She then stood up and turned, walking to the door. "Thank you, Wendy. I have to be going now. I-"

"*SIT DOWN*" Wendy said in a voice that was not her own.

It was a voice that reached deep into Alex's very being and filled her with sickly dread. A booming baritone of anger no human voice could make.

For a few moments, Alex stood facing her exit, while behind her, she heard a light squelching sound.

Spinning back to Wendy, Alex saw something that made it no longer possible to mask her shock. She had suspected that she was in the presence of the Djinn. But even though she thought this might have been the case, even though she ignored her rational doubt, and even though she felt in her soul that this was not Wendy, Alex's worst fears were confirmed when she looked at the place where the thing that had called itself Wendy sat. And despite Alex's suspicions, seeing what she now saw with her own eyes, Alex felt no less terrified.

Sitting where Wendy once sat, dressed in the same clothes, was the man from her vision. Demarest. On the table next to the empty glass, sat the face of Professor Wendy Derleth, in a pool of its own juices.

"Please sit," Demarest said.

Shaking her head, Alex stood wide-eyed in shock and horror. A few moments passed. Demarest simply sat, smiling at her, waiting for her to find her voice.

"Where is Wendy?" Alex asked, her voice quivering with a rising panic.

"Oh, she is in the bedroom," Demarest said, motioning with his hand. Alex turned toward the door that was slightly ajar. "But I would not go in there if I were you, she is very dead. Bit of a messy business, removing someone's face, you know?"

"You...murdered her," Alex said.

"What kind of monster do you take me for? I couldn't leave her alive without her face. I did the only humane thing. Though I did not kill her. That is not within my power."

"Then...*how* is she dead?"

"I thought the research would have made that clear? I cannot do anything unless I am asked to. Surely you know that by now."

Alex realized that he had just admitted that he could not harm her. "She didn't ask you to kill her. You lying-"

"The petulance emerges." Demarest's smile bared most of his illusory human teeth. "I showed her my true face."

Alex looked confused. Demarest pointed to his mask of a visage. "This is not mine either. You realize that, do you not?" Alex didn't reply, so he continued. "Her reaction was not entirely flattering. She became quite hysterical in fact. I merely enquired as to whether she wished for me to release her from her fear."

Though Alex tried her best to keep her composure, her rage and her sorrow started to fog her mind.

"You, my dear," he said as he stood, glancing down to regard the feminine garments he still wore, clinging tightly to his male body, "are a dangerous person to know. Most people close to you have been hurt. Your scientist friend. Your employer. The detective." He motioned toward the bedroom. "Her."

"Her name was Wendy."

"And her name is now damnation." The smile was a seemingly constant feature on his wicked face. "Now tell me, where is your pretty sister?"

"What are you asking?" she was barely able to reply.

Demarest caught a glimpse of his current human appearance in the mirror that hung over the fireplace.

"There is no more use for pretense, is there?" he said.

"Where is she?" Alex demanded, the emotion almost choking her words.

Demarest nodded, his hand raising to his face. With his fingers digging into the scalp, and with a disconcerting ease, he tore the human face from his own, revealing its true form. The male and female disguises were now gone. Its chest puffed out as the clothes that Wendy had once worn ripped open beneath its own grotesque physique. A swelling caused the human attire to fall onto the floor in shreds. A long hessian robe tumbled to the carpet from somewhere within its form. Its jagged ferocious teeth were now in place of the human ones. Its eternally dark eyes clouded the brightness of his human features. Its hands were clawed.

The Demarest face was still being held within one of the beast's clawed hands. He released it and it landed onto the carpet with a wet sickly sound.

Her body shaking, her nerves splitting, Alex witnessed this spectacle with mounting terror. The Djinn, now naked of all human disguise, stood as a vision of unadulterated horror.

And as he spoke, the demonic growl that emanated from his lips reinforced the fact that all traces of humanity had been abandoned. All that remained was its demonic growl. "The time for illusion is now over. Here I stand, as I am. Now, make your wishes."

Despite her choking fear, Alex shook her head defiantly.

"Think of the upside," it said as it took a step nearer. Its clawed hands palm-upward. "You get three wishes. Three wishes of your choosing which I have to grant you." Taking another step, it continued. Its long ancient robes dragged on the carpet, staining it a greasy black as it moved. "Doesn't that intrigue you? Fill you with the wonder of possibility? Even just a little? *Anything* you want. Anything!"

"Anything?" Alex asked. Her voice belied her determined expression.

"Anything your heart desires. The rules of nature do not apply here, nor do the laws of time and space. You ask me for anything, and I must grant it. Do you wish to explore the universe on a trail of stardust? I grant it. A trip to see the Pharaohs of Egypt? I grant it. To see the city of Atlantis, before its fall? I grant it. Riches? Fame? Fortune? Love? Granted. Granted. *Granted.* You need only wish."

"Right." Her voice had the same contempt that her face

now bore. "And what would I get in return for these wishes? Humanity laid to waste as you and your kind destroy us all."

"Then wish defensively. Wish yourself safe for the duration of your natural life." It had spoken such words of comfort to many humans in its past. Each and every one eventually relented.

"I don't play defensively," she said.

"Oh I forgot." It said, and laughed hideously. "You plan to match wits with me."

"What happens if I wish you dead? You said you cannot be killed. But what if I wish it? You said laws of nature do not apply here."

The Djinn snarled, placating Alex. "How remarkably original. I'll tell you what. I will offer you a free wish. A sample. To get you into the spirit of these proceedings. Is this acceptable?"

"Like I can trust you."

The placatory tone gone, the Djinn's hands fell to return to its side. Its eyes, though as black as the ones belonging to a shark, carried the look of one offended. "I do many things. Many things that your kind deem despicable, things you label as evil. But one thing I do not do - what I never do - is lie. I *cannot* lie to a summoner. I can trick and I can scheme, but I cannot lie. Not about this. Not about my very essence."

"Then I want you to kill yourself," she said resolutely. "Right now."

Without a heartbeat passing, the Djinn raised its hand. Within its clawed grasp now sat a large revolver - which the Djinn immediately raised to its temple, and fired a shot. The bullet exploded out of the gun's barrel, ripped its way through the creature's thick flesh, and burst out of the other side, leaving a large exit wound. Black blood gushed out from the wound, and onto the carpet. Spatter speckled the wall opposite where the bullet had embedded itself.

As fast as it was opened, this wound healed itself over, almost instantaneously, leaving no trace of the gun ever having fired a single shot.

The Djinn shrugged and smiled apologetically to Alex. "If it is of any consolation," it said slowly, "I can assure you that the pain I just endured was very, very real."

"You didn't kill yourself," she said, triumphantly, as if proving her earlier point.

"I did as you asked. Is it my fault if your wishes are half-formed? Barely even coherent? Vague and ill-conceived? If you leave me to fill in the gaps of your wishes, then that blame lays not with me."

In its hand, the gun slowly twisted itself of its own accord. The very molecules ripping themselves apart, then recombining. This weapon shifted its structure, color, and matter until it became a single, perfect rose.

Tossing it gently to Alex's feet, the beast said, "A token of my affection. Now, shall we continue?"

"I coach basketball," she said.

"Fascinating," it said, sarcastic. "Make your wishes."

"I always tell my girls to know their opponents. So I'll do as you ask. I'll ask you for one wish. One that can help me more than it can help you."

"This is new... What do you ask of me?" The intrigued tone in its voice was sincere. Its eyes fixed onto her - patient as a spider in the center of its web, waiting for a fly to fall into its trap.

"I wish," she began, careful of each word she uttered. "I wish to know what you are, where you come from, what makes you tick."

As she spoke, the Djinn brought the opal out from its robed pocket.

Presenting it outstretched on its palm, it held the gem out for Alex to see.

"What are you doing?" she asked.

With a smirk, the Djinn replied...

"As you wish..."

CHAPTER

# TWENTY

As her thoughts raced to make sense of what the stone was to the Djinn, beyond a prison, her vision flooded with a wash of the brightest, and most vivid red light that she could ever have imagined.

Finding herself standing in a strange corridor, Alex looked all around her, taking in the surroundings, as well as making sure she was not about to be attacked. The architecture here seemed similar to the angles on the surface of the opal. It was not only the same in structure, it was the same in color. She realized that all the vivid red light belonged to the stone.

A thought ran through her mind; the stone was more than just a prison a sorcerer had created. Alex had seen *through* its eye to those visions. It must be intrinsic to the Djinn's power.

In this corridor, in what she could only presume was a world within the gem itself, was where she presently stood. Somehow inside its strange and terrifying walls.

A world in crimson that reeked of the Djinn, not just the one that sometimes called itself Demarest, but as in the entire race of beings. She could sense them all somehow.

Feeling like Alice trapped in some dark Wonderland, she

continued walking. The corridor ahead of her wound its way round, turn after turn. She couldn't discern what was ahead at any point, or more pointedly, what was lying in wait behind each corner she approached.

She felt as if she were passing through the intestines of a giant, unspeakable beast.

Walking further down the corridor, a thick and oppressive breeze pushed by her. The stench in the air stung her nose as she tried to hold her breath to keep from vomiting.

The hallway came to an end, and she found he had emerged into the demonic throne room she'd been in before. The corpse-made throne at the head of the room, however, was empty this time. Unlike before, the human-disguised Djinn was not sitting there. This room existed in more of the same twisted style. The corridor was made of curved corners which turned so you could not see in a straight line for long. Though the cobblestone floor was flat, the walls curved upward to meet in the center above her head. The metal struts from the room before were here, in more of a semi-organic mixture of flesh and stone, yet still punctuated their walls equidistantly. The walls themselves were soft and translucent, a deep red glow throbbing from behind them. The walls rippled and pulsed, as if something unnatural had passed behind them, threatening to break their way out.

Unceasing, unpleasant sounds emanated out from every crease and corner of this structure. Sounds that beat, throbbed, and snarled. It was a river of noise that flowed too close for comfort.

As she looked around, a movement to the side drew her attention to the far walls. She then had the grim realization that she was not alone. Her eyes widened in terror as she saw the bodies of five people, each naked and bound to a different section of the wall; the victims of the Djinn, writhing under their bindings. Their mouths had been sewn shut, their screams muffled and barely audible over the sounds that emanated from behind the walls.

Though Alex did not recognize her in human form, Ariella, the young sales assistant, was hung on one wall section, strung up between two struts. Organic tentacles blossomed from the wall's fleshy surfaces, wrapped around her, then traced over her body as if tasting her. Between each stolen lick, they whipped her viciously.

On the next section of the wall, she saw Detective Nathanson, tied spread-eagle. His stomach flayed apart. The flaps of his skin torn back from his body, then embedded into the fleshy surface he seemed to be a part of. From inside of him, tendrils made their way in through his back and moved like snakes amongst his falling intestines, which themselves tumbled from his open gut into a stinking pile on the floor.

The next, the student, Charlie Villaraponster, had been crucified upside down on the next wall section. Tentacles burst through his wrists and ankles, keeping him in place in a horrific mocking of the crucifixion. All over his body, thousands of tiny cuts bled. Instead of obeying any rules of gravity, these cuts trickled their blood off the nearest curve of his body, then absorbed into the wall he was attached to. The whole wall behind him undulated as if the very surface was drinking his blood slowly. Drop by drop. Feeding on the poor boy's perpetual torment.

The homeless man also suffered a fate just as horrific. His whole body had been half-submerged within the wall itself, which unlike the other walls, was now gusting with a black steam. The fleshy substance this part of the wall was made of obviously boiled at an incredible heat. The poor man's flesh seared and burned repeatedly. As the skin turned black, it bubbled then crusted over. This damage soon dissolved, though, and the flesh became healthy again. It then repeated in the cycle. He was being cooked alive in the wall, over and over again.

Just when she thought she couldn't take anymore, her eyes turned to the last body. She tried to force herself to look away, but couldn't.

Nick.

He was held by tentacles protruding from his section of the wall. Each of his limbs was held in their vice-like grip. Every few moments, the tentacles shifted with unrelenting violence, sharply twisting around the part of the body it held - the bones within, snapping with a terrifying crack. Then a respite. Then, the same happened again back the way it came. And again. And again. The bones broke, moved back and healed. Then broke again.

She watched as a tentacle wrapped around his head, snapped his neck to the side, where it hung at a horrifying angle, then snapped back into its normal place, only to be done over again. His eyes clearly expressed the sheer torment he was under.

Though none of these prisoners' mouths could open, she could read the agony in their eyes. They all shared the same look. The look that said *Help us. For God's sake, help us.*

Looking away, Alex struggled to keep the tears from bursting out. Her lip trembled and she closed her eyes. These were the flashes of violence she had seen while in the hospital. She had witnessed each of these tortures.

A low laugh swam over the constant sound of this world's pounding inferno. A familiar voice. An unnatural voice.

Gritting her teeth, she opened her eyes, and looked at the Djinn now sitting on the throne of bodies. Using all her strength, she held firm, not allowing her fear to break the surface.

"You wanted to know what I am," it said. "I am this..." It paused dramatically. "The cry of the victim. The whimper of the whipped beast. The darkness that dwells beyond the reflection. I am the hollowness at the heart of all humanities hope. Alexandra Amberson, I am *manifest despair*."

Letting his words sink into the silent visitor's mind, the Djinn snapped its fingers.

From behind its throne, a monstrous shape - something half-animal and half-human - lunged forward.

It was a horrid, twisted grotesquery of a being. Screaming and growling at once, it looked up at its master, the Djinn, who returned its glance and smiled.

Upon this silent command from the Djinn, this slave-monster howled in a threatening fury. Alex caught a glimpse of the creature's cavernous maw. Half of its teeth were sharp, twisted fangs, while the other half seemed to be ordinary human teeth. It turned in her direction violently, then moved in on her. In a slithery crawl, it sped down the steps at her.

With a scream, she turned and ran from where she had come; back down the corridor.

"Be careful what you wish for," the Djinn said, calling after her.

Alex sprinted as fast she could, around the continuous turns of the corridor, unknowing that her pursuer only chased her to the entrance of the throne room. When the hell-beast had gotten to the edge of that room, it skidded to a halt, roared menacingly in a tormented howl that was, like its teeth, somehow both human and animalistic, then slid back into the shadowy recesses behind the throne where it had first emerged.

As she raced down the corridor, she hit a dead end. A wall. There was no path left except back the way she had come. This corridor seemed to exist unto itself. Not to join two rooms together, like a stationary appendage leading away from the throne room.

Turning around, she listened for a moment, waiting for the horrific roar of the monster chasing her. But after a few moments, she realized nothing was coming down the corridor.

Turning again, she examined the wall blocking her path. Putting her hand up to it, she felt its malleable consistency.

As she pushed harder with her hand, its softness started to give against her weight.

Jerking her hand back, she noticed a thick stringy mucus stretching between her palm and the wall. Disgust crept up her face.

The walls suddenly rippled, and Alex backed away in shock as she witnessed the fleshy substance in front of her start to ooze and move apart - almost as though birthing the Djinn.

"How are you enjoying your visit?" it said.

"I didn't wish you *here*. You're outside. How can you be here?"

Taking a moment, the Djinn's head tilted slightly to one side, considering something. "I have never met one of your kind who does not immediately beg. You are... interesting. But to answer your question, I am bound by that which I bind. Contained by that which I contain."

Alex looked back at the Djinn with equal parts hatred and confusion.

"I am that which is not. I am a paradox. I am *the* paradox. I do not expect your kind to understand the depth of our existence."

"This isn't what I wanted," she said. "I never asked for this."

His mouth curled into a sneer as he stepped forward. "You

may not be as weak as your kind, but you listen as well as they. Your wishes are *as you ask*. If they are not to your satisfaction, then word them more carefully. You wanted to know what I am, where I am from, *what makes me tick*." It raised its hands up, motioning to its surroundings. "*This*. It is through no fault of mine that you fail to understand."

Turning, the Djinn walked back toward the wall, where the surface parted again into a passageway through which it could travel. "Imagine an ant wished to know how humanity moved so far across the land, and you placed it inside an automobile. You think it would be satisfied with the answer?"

With that, the door sealed, and Alex heard a snarl behind her.

Spinning around, she saw one part of the wall up on the corner ahead. It started to swell - just as the wall did when the Djinn walked through it. This was not the Djinn, however; this was something *else*.

"Shit," was all Alex managed to say, before another portal blossomed into existence before her very eyes - this one exposing the Djinn's slave-monster, which now slithered through.

Realizing she was trapped in the corridor, she sprinted forward, toward the creature, and ducked out of the reach of the swinging clawed hand of the monster - which now half-hung out of the wall - as Alex ran on.

She ran down the twists and turns of the corridor for a third time. And yet, the walls she ran past now were different than before. New openings - like doorways - started to appear, as she sprinted in a fury, not daring to stop and look in. She could hear the slave-monster's roars getting closer behind her. She didn't dare look. She didn't dare turn. She only dared run.

She would get to the throne room soon.

*Then what?* she wondered in panic.

As she ran past the last corner, where the throne room *should* have been, there was only another dead end.

Then the wall itself opened up like a grotesque, retracting sphincter, showing a seemingly infinite space just beyond its translucent, solid membrane.

On the other side of the membrane, there was movement as a huge black eye came into focus - watching her. It was bigger than the entire opening.

*This was the Djinn looking into the gem from the outside.*

She covered her ears with her hands as its magnified laughter reverberated throughout this entire world, shaking the very foundations beneath her feet.

It spoke, and its voice boomed all around her. "Poor Alexandra. Stuck in another world. Such a pity she left her sister all alone. Perhaps I will find her? Keep her company for a time? Cater to her every...wish?"

"Don't you hurt her," Alex screamed at the eye. "Don't you fucking *dare* go near her!"

"I could offer her a wish. I could unleash a biblical torment on her. I could twist her world to become one with *mine.* You shall hear her screams from within my world. You'd be surprised at how persuasive the screams of loved ones can be."

"*NO!*" Her rage rang out as loud as his voice, the emotion seemingly shaking the walls.

"Then, my dear. Come back and stop me. Wish yourself back into your own world."

Alex had no other choice.

This monster had outsmarted her.

"I wish to be back in my apartment, right now!" she screamed. "Without you!"

# CHAPTER
# TWENTY-ONE

Back in her apartment, Alex stood in the middle of her darkened kitchen. In a panic, she glanced around hurriedly. Everything seemed to be normal here - but that didn't quell her concern that this may very well be a trick.

She quickly thought about her previously spoken words to see if she could find a hole in her phrasing - a way for him to fuck with her, to twist the wish into something that he could manipulate.

*I wish to be back in my apartment, right now*, she again thought to herself. *Without you.*

Could it have made her appear here in another time? Or one in another reality? No. Everything looked as it should.

*Shannon!*

Moving at speed, Alex ran through the apartment, into the living room.

"Shannon?" she called out, "Shannon?" She checked every part of her home where her sister could have been. Bathroom? No. Bedroom? No. Balcony? No.

Walking back into the living room, she caught sight of a

handwritten note next to the phone. In Shannon's writing it said:

*Alex,*

*Gone to Beaumont's party. I hope you're okay. I'm worried. I'm here if you need me. Please take a pill.*

A sigh of relief.

*Thank God*! Alex thought to herself.

She then noticed the answering machine flashing, and saw there was a message waiting. She pressed play. Demarest's voice - that familiar adopted tone of the Djinn - oozed from the speaker. "Two wishes in. Have you learned anything yet?" She could hear its awful smile in every word. "We are connected now. Wherever you go, there I will be too. We are linked. Now... If you do not mind. I have a party to get to."

With a laugh and a click, the recording stopped.

Grabbing the car keys from the glass bowl by the door, Alex rushed out of the apartment.

Moments later, she was racing through the lamp-lit city streets, her foot barely off the accelerator as she barreled through a red light. She didn't care at this moment. She *had* to get to the party. She *had* to protect Shannon.

Other drivers on the road angrily honked their horns at Alex as she spun around corners, not stopping for anything.

She ignored the many passing shouts of abuse from the pedestrians as she cut off their attempted paths across the street. She drove regardless of anything else around her. Her eyes fixed ahead. Singularly focused. Knowing where she had to go: Deep in the *stillness* of her mind she had taught her team about so often.

One thing she had learned from her time inside the

Djinn's 'gemworld', was that it was not *just* a stone. The sorcerer must have first received the gem from the Djinn somehow, as it was not only a source of the Djinn's power, but from what she could guess, an intrinsic part of its whole race. Being trapped inside was, for the Djinn (as much as she could fathom) like being trapped inside your own body.

Gunning the car through a large intersection, Alex drove on. She had left the lower-income part of town behind her, and she sped through the business district and onto the more well-to-do residences. The houses on these roads started to get bigger, more luxurious. Weeds and litter gave way to greenery and country clubs. With each block she had driven by, the prices of the homes jumped by hundreds of thousands of dollars.

Far ahead, at an intersection, the lights started to turn red. Flooring it, Alex tried her best to beat the change, but it turned red long before she got close. The cross-traffic quickly blocked her path as their light turned green. She slammed on her brakes and skidded to a stop, just over the traffic line. A few feet short of the crossing cars.

Stopped at a slight angle, Alex's breathing was stilted and nervous as the adrenaline raced through her.

"Going my way?"

Demarest's voice grabbed her attention. She turned and saw him out of the passenger window. There he stood, human again, complete with his fine suit and coiffured hair.

"I told you, I would *always* be right behind you," he said, never once dropping his smug grin, as he walked across the road toward the car. He held his hand out, ready to grab the door handle.

Without a second thought, Alex floored the accelerator. The wheels screeched as they spun on the asphalt, before gaining traction and propelling her forward - out of his grip.

Swerving into the traffic that moved ahead of her, she weaved with miraculous luck between the other cars; escaping unharmed as at least three other cars collided with each other.

Demarest knew she was lucky he was there, or she may have met her end in a collision, like those left in her wake. He couldn't allow her to die. She needed to die by his rules, or not at all. Ever.


In the car, driving up to the large facade of Beaumont's estate, Alex sped through its open double gates; the valets unable to slow her arrival. They could only watch aghast as she raced up the drive, toward the hidden house - where the party was in full swing.

Where she would find Shannon.

# Stillness in Crimson

# TWENTY-TWO

Alex slammed the car to a screeching halt. Despite her hurry and lack of focus on anything except the matter at hand, she noticed how opulent the mansion looked tonight. The driveway had been lit by flaming torches, and the house itself was bathed in the kind of lighting reserved for an awards show or film premiere.

Flinging the driver's side door open, with the car keys absent-mindedly left in the ignition, she flung herself out, and headed for the steps which led to the main entrance.

"My dear," said a vile voice from behind her.

Her veins ran cold. She turned and saw Demarest leaning against her car, leg casually crossed at the ankles. He gave her a little wave as, with the other hand, he spun her car keys on one of his fingers. "You left these behind."

He threw the keys, and she caught them with ease, never breaking eye contact.

"There is no escape," he said. "Make your wish. Save us both."

She turned and rushed up the stairs, where she was immediately stopped by a tuxedo-clad doorman - a tall imposing figure - whose professionally impassive face didn't quite mask the quiescent strength of what he really was; a seasoned urban warrior.

"Hold on there," he said in a voice so stern, despite its non-threatening tone, that it made her stop and stare in compliance.

"Please," she said, making to move inside. The doorman moved to stand in her way.

"Can I have your name, ma'am?"

How could she explain this to anyone? *Oh a supernatural old evil is chasing me to make a third wish, but I don't want to, or else the world will be destroyed by his kind, which he will bring here with his magic stone.*

"For God's sake, please help me. Please. This guy-" She motioned to Demarest, still leaning on her car. "Don't let him in. He's my stalker. He's dangerous."

The doorman looked up and saw Demarest, who pushed himself off from the car, and headed up the steps.

"My name is Alex Amberson. Please."

The doorman's attention stayed on Demarest.

Alex had tried his chivalrous side, now she would try his professional one. "He's not even invited here."

With a raised eyebrow and a small nod, the doorman moved out of her way, letting her pass. With a sigh of relief, Alex rushed inside to find her sister.

Stepping forward, the doorman addressed Demarest as soon as he was a few paces away. "Excuse me, sir. Is Mister Beaumont expecting you tonight?"

Demarest didn't even make eye contact with the burly man. He kept walking as if the hired muscle was beneath his contempt.

Throwing an arm out, the doorman grabbed Demarest by his shoulder. "I asked you a question," the doorman said.

Staring at the hand now on his shoulder, Demarest looked as if he could not believe that a human had the audacity to touch him.

Demarest held his hands up and stood back, realizing that this problem would need to be addressed. Ignoring the affront would not be possible.

"My apologies," Demarest said through his smile.

"Are you expected?" the doorman said again, now in rising irritation.

Demarest locked eyes with the doorman. "Am I expected?" Not blinking, not looking away. "Yes. If this Beaumont has ever had a nightmare, if he has ever felt fear, if he has ever worried about feeling the cold hand of death near him - then he has always expected me."

"Halloween ain't for a while," the doorman said, unimpressed. He had heard it all before. Having worked everything from strip clubs to government residences, he had heard *every excuse* any idiot could invent. "While it might sound impressive that you haunt his dreams, it don't sound like no invitation to this event."

With no trace of his usual amusement, Demarest sneered at the doorman as he said, "I don't care what it sounds like. And I don't care to be impeded by a slave dressed in fineries. Get out of my way!"

"Let me make this simple." The bouncer squared up to Demarest. The doorman was a full foot taller than Demarest, and double the weight in pure muscle. "If you are not on the list, then the only place you will go is out."

Looking up at his new adversary, Demarest matched the doorman's glare, unphased. "I have dealt with your type before."

Demarest remembered the guard he'd recently eviscerated at the auctioneer house.

Though the doorman could not tell what Demarest was thinking, he heard the contempt in the man's voice. The Doorman's eyes turned to ice as he spoke low and precisely to the smaller man, enunciating each word with a threatening tone. "Boy. You ain't *never* met my type before."

Taking a step back, Demarest took a moment. He did not have time for this, but he may as well have some fun nonetheless.

"There is more at stake here than your feeble brain could possibly understand," Demarest said. He looked at the doorman with sincerity. "Here is all you need to know: I am going through that door. And, if you value what life you have, you will stand aside. Do I make myself clear, *servant*?"

The doorman put the clipboard down on a nearby window ledge, and let his arms fall to his side. They spread a little from his body, and his fingers flexed - a small gesture but one that spoke volumes of his knowledge of violence. "I want you to remember my face. Remember it after they ask you how you lost your eyes."

Demarest laughed. "Are you threatening *me*?"

"No sir," the doorman replied, his voice even and considered. "I am merely appraising you of the possible consequences of your dumbass actions."

Demarest was amused by this behemoth's display of fortitude. "Perhaps my eagerness for the endgame has skewed my judgment. Why don't we make a deal?"

"I don't make deals."

"I can make it worth your while."

"I don't take bribes either." His voice carried a tone of finality with every word.

"Then if I may ask..." Demarest's smile broadened as he stepped closer. "What do you do?"

"I keep assholes out of parties."

"Today perhaps, but what of tomorrow?" The smile didn't falter. "And the days following."

"My tomorrow isn't your problem." The doorman was getting tired of this party-crasher.

"It doesn't have to be your problem. Don't tell me this job is all you can do. It is certainly not all you have ever dreamed of."

The doorman said nothing. Not even a glint in his eye gave away his thoughts.

Demarest continued. "Tell me the truth; don't you tire of the shackles of a dreary job like this? The bindings of this work. Wouldn't you like something more exciting. Something more than just being stuck here, speaking to the likes of me?" He leaned into the guard and said with a whisper. "Wouldn't you rather try to escape?"

"What the fuck has it got to do with you?" The doorman had had enough. He grabbed Demarest by the collar.

"Me? Nothing. Or Everything. Take a chance. Answer the question. Answer, and I will do what you ask, then I will leave you."

The doorman wasn't stupid. If this asshole had a chance of leaving just by being humored, it would be better than bloodying up yet another shirt.

"Would I like to? Sure. Why not?" he said.

After a moment, Demarest nodded his head to the doorman.

"As you wish..."


Demarest walked toward the door, and over the spot where the doorman had stood a few moments ago.

A terrible muffled scream came from behind Demarest. At his back, there now stood a large iron-framed water tank. The doorman, wrapped tightly in a weighted straitjacket, was completely submerged in the water, eyes wide in panic as he struggled desperately to break free.

Addressing the doorman before walking into the party, Demarest said, "Houdini did it in two-and-a-half minutes. See if you can beat that time."

CHAPTER

# TWENTY-THREE

Entering the ballroom, Alex glanced around as she tried to spot her sister. The large room was crowded with some of the city's most respected and wealthy elite. From art collectors to futures traders, CEOs to government officials, the attendees comprised a veritable *Who's Who* of the most influential movers and shakers the city had to offer. Beaumont's Rolodex had no doubt been used to its full effect.

Around and throughout the room, some of his collected antiquities were on display, moved here from the various points throughout his mansion to allow the guests to marvel and drool in jealousy at their host's taste and wealth all in one room.

Each of the guests drank exquisite cocktails and ate haute cuisine hors d'oeuvres from the trays of milling waiters and waitresses.

At the far end of the room, a string quartet provided a tranquil backdrop of classical soundscapes. All pieces had been painstakingly chosen; all tasteful and composed by the quills of only the finest composers.

While searching the room for Shannon, Alex saw Beaumont - who had been talking to a group of eager listeners. He caught her attention and made a move toward her. Instead of staying to converse, she waved distractedly, then moved further into the crowd. For a brief moment, he appeared dejected, but soon turned his attention to other guests he could impress with his wealth.

Pushing forward, Alex weaved her way through the throng of people, feeling vastly underdressed in her t-shirt and jeans combo. She tried to not focus on anyone she may know from within the art community, or her job itself. There were a few times she had heard her name called by people she had no wish to talk to, and each time feigned ignorance, carrying on as if she hadn't heard a thing.

Approaching the large table in the middle of the room, Alex looked up at the huge centerpiece; an elaborate ice sculpture. In keeping with the garish tone of much of Beaumont's collection, it was in itself an abstract work, studded all throughout with long shards of metal; each piece was jagged and cruel-looking, and they skewered through the central ice column, like a torture device made of frozen steel. She turned away. It was too garish a sight for her.

Suddenly she spotted the back of Shannon's head. Alex ran up to her, and grabbed her by the shoulder.

"Shannon, don't ask questions, but we have to..." Her words fell away as the woman turned. It was not Shannon, just a stranger with the same bountiful curls.

Confused and annoyed, Alex mumbled an apology, then moved on.

*Dammit, where is she?*

As she continued her journey, Alex finally saw her sister. Shannon stood alone at the bar, looking better than Alex had ever seen her. Shannon's bohemian style was gone for the night, and was instead replaced by a classic black dress.

"Shannon," Alex called out, rushing over.

With a mixture of relief that her sister was okay, and worry that Alex may cause a scene, Shannon offered a calming smile. "I didn't think you'd show. After the hospital—"

"I'm fine. Better. Really. I know you're worried about me." Alex took the drink from Shannon's hand and placed it back on the bar.

"What are you doing?" Shannon said, annoyed.

"Getting you out of harm's way."

Shannon stared at her older sister blankly. This *again*. This *shtick*. Alex wasn't better at all. Just more deluded than ever.

Alex grabbed Shannon's arm, ready to lead her away, but Shannon knocked her hand aside.

"Fucking hell," Shannon whispered, angry. "You collapsed at home, then at the hospital, you start talking of demons coming to get you. You nearly have a fucking panic attack in the parking lot. Then you disappear without even telling me where you went. Now..." She motioned to Alex's clothes. "You turn up to this party like *this*. I don't mean to say 'what the fuck', Alex, but seriously, what the actual *goddamn* fuck?"

Alex stared at her sister. She was right. Alex had given her no reason to believe she was anything but mad, but she had to try and convince her otherwise. This was no joke. This was life and death. *Shannon's* life and possible death.

"I am *so* sorry," Alex said, "but if you ever believed anything I have ever said, believe me now. We *have* to leave. Trust me. Something *bad* is coming."

"Oh Jesus, *really*? No, Alex. I'm staying. Something bad is *not* coming tonight. Something good *may* be coming, though. And I have my eye on *who* that something good could be."

Alex noticed that Shannon's gaze was directed over Alex's shoulder. Following it, Alex saw it went to the other side of the ice sculpture, where Beaumont now stood, chatting to a good-looking, well-dressed man.

Demarest.

Full of smiles and laughter, as ever.

"Who is your friend, Mr. Beaumont?" Shannon said quietly to herself.

"...and I was at Cindy's party, of course." Beaumont was saying, attempting to impress his new guest by proving himself a true raconteur. "The one where they served the divorce papers in the middle of dinner. It was hysterical. The talk of the scene for months!"

Demarest laughed believably, while inside he longed to eviscerate Beaumont along with the entire crowd.

"Only months?" Demarest said. "Really? I remember a certain potentate whose party was talked about for centuries. Wouldn't take much for yours to be the same."

Alex was horrified to see the monster inside the building. Seeing him converse with Beaumont filled her with dread. Turning back to the bar, she found that Shannon had slipped away from her and had pushed through the crowd.

Alex followed after her, trying to navigate through the scores of people in her way.

. . .

"What do you mean," Beaumont asked his guest, "it made the history books?"

Demarest smiled, "It was legendary." As he spoke, he scanned the crowd, looking for his summoner.

"Oh man," Beaumont said, wistfully. "I'd love for my party to be remembered like that. Wouldn't take much, you say? Well, if you know how, I'd love to see it happen."

Then, Demarest spotted Alex across the room, and without even looking at Beaumont, he replied, the gleefully slick words falling from his lips.

"As you wish..."

And just like the court of the Persian king, Beaumont's party instantly descended into a nightmarish chaos. Bodies reconfigured into a whirl of transmuting flesh and bloodied screams.

A female guest holding a cocktail glass watched in terror as her hand started to turn into the same material it held; her flesh, inch by inch, giving up its fleshly consistency in favor of crystalline solidity, as she, too, was becoming made of glass. So fast a consumption, in fact, that she tried to scream, but by the time she pulled the breath into her lungs, the glass had already overtaken them, leaving her frozen in eternal anguish, as it continued to consume the rest of her body.

Alex ran from one group of scattering people right into the glass woman, and knocked her to the floor. The woman smashed into thousands of pieces, leaving the small parts of her body which were still flesh twitching angrily on the floor, as each remnant of flesh piece slowly completed its transformation; the onset of death doing nothing to abate her cursed death.

Alex was caught in the middle of this hellish storm. Terrified to see the myriad of horrors happening around her.

Next to her, a waiter screamed when antlers burst

bloodily from his head, and his hands shredded apart as they exposed newly sprouting hooves. In only a few more steps, his entire body broke apart in a mass of gore, letting a terrified-looking deer loose into the crowd. This panicky, gore-soaked animal savagely bucked and gored people with its horns as it sought escape.

Alex watched as a male guest grabbed the arm of a female guest in sheer panic, hoping to grasp onto anything to steady him as he witnessed the carnage.

When his hand touched this woman, her body - in the blink of an eye - transformed into an exact double of the man in every physical way. The dress she still wore being the only difference. The clone turned toward the male guest with a wicked grin.

As the man's eyes drank in the uncanny replica, he staggered backward in terror, bumping into a family that was trying to make their own escape. Turning to face those he collided with, the man saw that they, too, had transformed into copies of him. This family of replicas; one in a dress, one in a suit, and one in now shredded child-sized clothes - all shared the same wicked grin as the first woman who had been changed.

Holding out their arms, these copies touched more of the fleeing guests, their gaze never breaking with the terrified man. In turn, their touch caused more and more people to transform in an instant, only to stop again, and turn toward the man and offer the same grin.

It was when the number got to about fifty, that the copies stopped replicating, and they all advanced on the man; their expressions full of gleeful malevolence. They licked their lips hungrily as they crowded around him.

They hungered for *him*. For his flesh.

Before he could even try to escape, each one of his copies

all leaped upon him. Ripping at him with their hands. Biting into him with their grinning mouth. These corrupt and cannibalistic knock-offs were like a pack of rabid dogs, tearing at their prey.

Soon though, there was no more left to tear apart; the remnants of his body, no longer anything except a pile of broken bones and guts. When this feeding frenzy slowed, the copies turned on each other - all cannibalizing and tearing at each other in a wild fury. One by one these copies fell from their injuries, as they consumed and ate each other to death.

Getting to her feet, looking at the shattered glass on the floor, Alex found herself in a panic when she realized that Shannon was nowhere to be seen; only impossible corruption all around her. Everywhere she looked, people were either running from imminent death, or screaming in its throes.

Turning at the sound of a blood-curdling scream, Alex saw a man that had fallen to his knees, one hand on the central table - steadying himself. She watched as metal from the ice sculpture shot out, splintering into needle-like shards, and burrowed into his body. The piercing needles moved of their own accord, twisting and moving throughout the man's body, like mice scrambling to escape a maze. They had entered, and were now looking for any escape they could, any way they could. Some protruded from his eyes, some from his groin. It took an unnatural amount of time for the man to finally collapse, lifeless. As if only the torture itself had been keeping him alive out of some sentient sadism.

Turning back, Alex closed her eyes tight, shutting out this nightmare. She was safe, she had to remind herself. He wouldn't hurt her until she made her wish.

One of the violinists from the string quartet lay on the floor, his throat flayed by his own bow - which moved in the air, trying to play a tune on his exposed windpipe. Choking on his own blood, his gargling was the only tune that could be heard.

The grand piano at one end of the room played insanely fast melodies of its own - a dozen concertos chiming simultaneously. As it reached a crescendo, the strings from inside burst free from their positions deep in the piano's belly and flew across the room like murderous razor wire.

Some of these strings whipped the fleeing guests, splitting skin like a large scalpel, then dismembered them, leaving body parts tumbling to the floor. If any of the victims had not been cut down by a first attack, the strings returned to finish their work in the second, or third.

The pianist had cowered underneath his piano ever since it had become possessed. He thought himself safe, but the strings soon found him. When they did, they wrapped around his wrist and face - sinking deeply into the flesh and bone - blood erupting as the strings tightened themselves. Another string dragged him out into the open, far away from his hiding place. In one, slow, grotesque movement, the string wrapped around his throat and, slowly - very slowly - cut into his skin in a coiling motion, like a boa constrictor with its meal. At last, the strings decapitated him, slicing through his spinal cord. They could have made quick work of the man, but instead the wires, seemingly deliberately, took their time.

A woman in a strapless gown furiously scratched at a red spot that appeared on her shoulder. In a panic, she became too focused on her own torment to notice all the unthinkable horrors happening around her. As the spot on her shoulder swelled, it grew larger and larger, until it finally burst open. A monstrous insect scuttled out of the wound; a mixture of a centipede and tarantula with a grotesque face housing vicious fangs. Shaking itself free from the amniotic pus, it was followed by another just like it. When they had both emerged, they turned, at speed, on their terrified mother, and spat an acidic venom into her face, burning her on impact as the venom started to dissolve her skin. Within seconds, the venom had left her skull exposed, and her eyeballs had melted away. Nothing she could do abated the savage attack of her insect children.

As more people screamed in absolute panic, hoping to find any means of escape, Beaumont stood in mortal terror. While everyone scattered, he looked around for any sign that this was not really happening. Surely, this was some kind of wildly elaborate joke at his expense, right?

He turned to the well-dressed man he had been speaking to, but the man was nowhere to be seen. In his place, however, was a hideous, imposing creature dressed in a hessian robe.

It was the Djinn, and his clawed hand held the face of the man Beaumont had been addressing.

"Oh my God," Beaumont said, his voice choked by all-consuming horror.

The Djinn smiled as he pointed his finger at Beaumont. "Soon, mortal. Soon I *will* be. My brethren and I shall walk on the remnants of your race."

As the nightmare party raged on, the jetting piano wires continually flailed about, decimating anyone they could; capturing some for slower, and slower kills.

One screaming man was picked up by the feet, then hurled into the piano. The lid slammed down onto his body as if it were a large mouth. Inside the piano, the man's body was crushed to pulp as the weight of the lid repeatedly pummeled his fragile bones.

Everywhere, people were either dead, dying, or still fruitlessly running for their lives, bloodied and bruised.

Alex had escaped unharmed physically. Mentally, however, she had seen so much death, she knew it would be a miracle for her to escape with her sanity intact.

Suddenly she saw her sister, who was being swept along by part of the crowd at the rear of the room, into an annex located at the side of Beaumont's ballroom.

Fighting to follow, Alex was stopped by an explosive sound.

Out of the fireplace in front of her, a massive jet of flames leaped outward, as if a dragon had been lying in wait. The flame billowed out, blocking her path, engulfing some survivors, and consuming them in seconds. Those who didn't fall, continued to run in a dying panic, colliding with others, confused and blinded, as they set fire to everything and everyone they touched.

One flaming victim rushed straight past Alex, through a plate glass window that led out into Beaumont's gardens. Howling, and with the fresh cuts over his burning body, the flaming man ran as far as he could before finally succumbing to his injuries a few feet from the tree line.

Avoiding the flames, Alex hurried into the annex.

As she got to the entrance, she went from panicked to aghast.

The annex was full of art and antiquities. Modern paintings, ancient sculptures and vice versa. Though it was not these clashes of periods which affected Alex; it was the sheer amount of corpses. There were a multitude of freshly slain bodies; human lives laid to waste in the same amount of time it had taken the fireplace to belch fiery death.

A moment ago, this was a room that a stampeding crowd had run into.

Now it was a room full of corpses, not just on the floors, but hanging off every bit of art and furniture. Blood and gore coated everything, even the ceiling was not spared. Like a wave of pure carrion had flowed through here, leaving nothing untouched in its wake.

Moving in cautiously, Alex could only focus on her need to find Shannon. She refused to believe that Shannon could be numbered amongst the dead. Alex had to find her.

She scanned the room as she walked gingerly over the dead bodies. The screams from the ballroom faded into the distance the further she went.

As she approached the halfway mark, Alex gasped at a clump of tentacles she saw suddenly twitching at her, reaching for her. They squealed as they protruded from the severed throat of a deceased female guest, who had been impaled upside down onto a twisted modern art sculpture.

Then, a familiar sound behind her caused her to turn and look back in the direction from which she had come.

Walking in from the ballroom, the Djinn appeared. With a look of victory on its demonic face, it headed her way, never dropping that *stupid fucking never-ending smile.* As if it was celebrating a victory before it had even won. God, how she wanted to wipe it off its smug face. The Djinn was clearly in no hurry. Each step he took was purposeful and menacing.

Alex stood next to a sculpture that she had recognized as the sea-god Triton, whose stone-carved face seemed to stare at the Djinn with appropriate hatred and fear, as it held a trident aloft in its hand.

"We have unfinished business, my dear," the Djinn said.

"And it'll stay unfinished!"

Motioning to the room at its back, the Djinn never took its eyes off her. "Listen to that melody. Listen to the music they make."

"You bastard!" she screamed.

"I am guessing, then, you do not find it as soothing as I."

He stopped a dozen feet from her. "You can save them, you know? Just wish it undone, and it shall be so."

"I won't!" she said. "I can't!"

"You *should* and you *could*," it said, chuckling, "but if not that, then wish for anything else. And please, do it quickly. Before my patience fully expires."

Getting braver, she took a step forward, away from the shadow of Triton. "What are you gonna do?" she said, hatred in her voice. "Are you gonna kill me? What the hell's gonna happen to your third wish then?"

"Oh, child. I do not need or want you dead. I just need you to wish that you were."

It loosed a hellish laugh, and as if on cue, the statue of Triton next to her moved, the stone cracking and screeching as it did so. The statue threw its trident toward Alex, missing her face by inches, embedding itself deeply in the wall to the other side of her. Screaming in shock, she scrambled backward, further into the annex.

As she ran, a painting by Picasso shuddered itself into life. A creature from a cubist nightmare - a horror of bright colors and disjointed limbs - stepped off from the canvas and lunged at her.

Opposite, a bronze octopus slithered from its plinth, its suckered limbs twitching and grabbing hungrily for Alex.

As Alex reached the door into the adjoining corridor, a momentary blindness consumed her as a Jackson Pollock action painting erupted from its framed confines and swirled around her like a snowstorm of different colors and shades. The abstract fluidity of this art was ineffective in its attack, as her arm swung through its paint with ease, sending it spinning off to another part of the room.

Without glancing back at her oncoming attackers, Alex ran through the corridor at the other end.

In a blind panic, Alex had escaped and run without looking back. She ran through room after room, corridor after corridor, trying her best to lose anything hot on her tail. Once, she finally got the nerve to look back, and, thankfully, could not see any monster or hideous creation following her.

She passed a side table with an oversized glass vase resting on it, and a figure turned the corner ahead, running into her. The figure grabbed her by the arm.

"*Get off me!*" Alex said.

It was Beaumont. He looked a fraction of the man he once had been.

"Alex, what are you doing here? I thought—"

His words were suddenly replaced by a violent choking and he quickly doubled over in agony. His body convulsed violently.

Backing away, Alex knew she couldn't do anything to help him, not without endangering Shannon. All she could do was witness, helplessly, as his body contorted. His back arched until it cracked. He vomited an impossibly large mass of writhing tentacles.

One of the tentacles jetted out - its base still deep within Beaumont's body - and grabbed Alex's ankle. As it pulled her to the floor, it dragged her nearer.

Then the other tentacles all reached to grab hold of her.

Beaumont's body was now a lifeless husk, housing these creatures like a grotesque hermit-crab, and they pulled him around while attacking Alex

Knocking into the side table, she tried to grab hold of something, anything. The oversized glass vase tumbled from on top and crashed onto the tentacle-driven Beaumont-creature.

Alex managed to kick away her fleshy bindings and crawl backward as she got to her feet.

Without wasting a moment, she charged through an adjacent door, wondering if this nightmare would ever end and if she would be still breathing when it did.

# CHAPTER
# TWENTY-FOUR

The late Anthony Beaumont (Born Bertram Beaumont), as all who knew him well enough realized, was not only a man whose wealth exceeded most of the city's gross domestic product combined, but he was also a man who knew a lot about the art he owned, and very little about any art that he did not.

Throughout his house sat millions upon millions of dollars' worth of art, accrued over his four-decade-long obsession. This started the same month as the mysterious and untimely deaths of everyone in his family, which had left young Bertram the sole heir to a fortune that could - and did - buy him anything and everything he wanted. When his father had been alive, Bertram was only given what he viewed as a pittance each month - a high five-figure pittance which Bertram considered as an insult. An insult that gave him no choice but to *save up* to buy things he wanted: something Bertram resented and hated his parents for.

His father's death was the best thing to happen to Bertram, and the best thing he had ever purchased. Of course it also came at the cost of the lives of his sister and mother, but he had thought them expendable.

On the first night of his newly found freedom, newly inherited wealth, and newly empty mansion, Bertram felt - for the first time - alone. Totally alone. He had sold everything that had belonged to his family so that their ghostly memories would not be reflected in the decor - including his father's entire art collection; something his father loved more than his own son. Bertram even fired the staff he had known his entire life.

But in the firelight of this empty mansion, Bertram became filled with regret. The callousness of what he had done finally hit him with the force of a freight train.

The only thing he did keep was his father's diary; a book which was almost a memoir of the man's life as an art collector.

Secluding himself in the mansion for months, Bertram Beaumont sank into a deeper and deeper depression as he read his father's diary over and over - until something happened, something most unexpected. One morning, Beaumont woke from a night of maudlin alcohol indulgence while reading his father's word, walked over to the still-burning fireplace, then cast the book into its flames. Then, he walked out of the house, and disappeared for three days.

When he returned, he had a new closely-cropped haircut - like his father's. A new wardrobe of tweed and cotton - like the one his father wore. A dozen pieces of art - like his father would have collected. And a new name - the name of his father: Anthony Beaumont.

Bertram was dead. He had died that night. And the man now called Anthony Beaumont never again dwelled on the man he used to be.

His father's art obsession had become his own, but the new Anthony Beaumont wanted *his* collection to eclipse anything that his father once owned. If it was expensive and rare, Beaumont needed it. And when he got it, he committed every morsel of information about it to memory, ready to regurgitate at any opportunity, to any interested party.

It was a great irony that this man, who housed a murderer behind a false veneer, would end up in possession of a statue that also contained a murderer within its own polished facade. If Beaumont had never murdered his family, the evil within the statute would have remained trapped within its clay confines, and it would never have been the cause of the end of Beaumont's life.


Alex ran into what Beaumont had called his 'Warrior Room'. Alex slowed when she was confronted with the life-sized statues of a quartet of ancient warriors: a gladiator, a samurai, a Mongol archer, and a Hindu warrior. She moved cautiously around these statues, as she was afraid they may spring to life and attack her, like other art pieces had.

Eyeing the statues, She recognized the gladiator, as she had been the one to appraise it, and had written in the report that it was an expertly forged remake of a genuine statue currently held in the Vatican vault. When she had informed him of this, he had laughed, saying, 'Well then, it will have to do until they sell me the real one'.

It was a tense, silent walk as her eyes fixed to these stone beings, not trusting their lifelessness.

She heard her own breath growing louder in the silence, and quickly tried to stifle it.

She made it to the far end of the room, where she heard a

panicked scuffle. Seven of the security guards who had been on duty suddenly rushed into the room, guns drawn; all coated in blood, which slicked down their black uniforms. Blood which was not theirs. They looked terrified and shocked by what they had experienced tonight. They spotted Alex at the other side of the statues, and one of the guards called out, "Hey miss, you okay?"

All of them walked further in; brave in words and deeds, but wearing the expressions of frightened children.

Walking calmly between the gladiator and the samurai statues, the guard who had called to her lowered his gun, and repeated, "Miss?"

Alex had no time to answer; her mouth just hung aghast as she saw the samurai's head turn to look at the guard.

"Get out!" Alex said. "You have to get out!"

Raising his hand to Alex in a calming gesture, another guard attempted to smile - a tough act after all the death they had recently observed.

He said, "It's okay. Come with us. We're here to help y-"

His words (and life) were cut immediately short as a stone arrow ripped through his face, demolishing his placatory smile into a twisted, ripped mess of bone, brains and blood.

The other guards looked around in terrified confusion, guns wildly pointing everywhere.

The Mongol archer reached for a second arrow, as the Hindu warrior and the gladiator stepped down from their plinths.

"Jesus fuck!" one guard exclaimed as the samurai leaped to the floor in front of him, and in one speedy, exact motion, sliced the guard's throat wide open.

Another guard raised his gun and fired at any and all of the attacking stone warriors, emptying his entire clip of bullets at them. Each bullet, though, had little effect; they merely blasted chips from these statues' cold, solid flesh.

Before the guard could reload, the Hindu warrior crushed his skull with its mallet.

Two of the other guards ran at speed to where Alex had sought safety - hoping to escape the immediate onslaught. The other remaining guards were not so lucky, they clustered together in the center of the room as the statues closed in on them.

The gladiator stood above one cowering guard, who fired his gun at it repeatedly. Impervious to the bullets, the gladiator raised its stone sword and thrust it down into the guard's chest.

The last guard in the open ran toward the exit - the way they came in - as the four statues turned to follow, blocking Alex's view of the doorway. Though terrified, she was selfishly relieved they had not seen or attacked her, while simultaneously half-crippled with the guilt she felt for knowing that she could end their pain. It would take a single request to the Djinn to stop all of this. But she couldn't give up. Not now. Not after everything she had been through. She knew there had to be a way out of this. She just needed more time.

In unison, before the stone monstrosities had walked two paces, they stopped, and all noise in the room ceased with them, including the screams of the escaping guard.

A low laugh emanated from the doorway.

A deep, unholy laugh.

The stone warriors parted to show the Djinn, smiling; his foot standing in the crushed remnants of the runaway guard's skull.

"Aren't you and your friends going to run too, my dear?"

The Djinn clearly found itself amusing. Alex wasted no

time, and backed through a side door, into a corridor, and was followed closely by the remaining two guards.

"What the fuck is happening?" one of the guards said, just before another arrow flew in from the other room and, with a *thwack*, burst through his stomach, sending his innards outward.

Stepping into the corridor, the archer had already reloaded his weapon. Aiming it at the falling guard, the archer fired the arrow, sending it flying at him. It pierced the guard's hand and pinned him to the wall; leaving his legs dangling, half-buckled on the floor.

Alex and the last guard backed up.

Neither of them saw, to their left, the dark and ominous painting; a shadowed Victorian gentleman looking out from the oils it had been created in. One hand held an elegant walking stick; the other, a medical bag.

Before Alex and the last guard could take another step, the Victorian gentleman leaped out from its canvas - leaving the painting to display only the dark streets the impasto fiend had once stood on. This attacker was semi-incorporeal to the eye; his skin and clothing a mass of disconnected, swirling oil paints. With its walking stick, it somehow smashed the guard across the scalp, sending him crashing to the marble floor.

Alex, denied the horror that tried to rip her from her sanity, and she backed away. She retreated hurriedly, and the half-made Victorian gentleman, now standing over his fallen victim, glanced at Alex, cast his walking stick to the floor, then smiled as it looked back down at the guard. The impossible thing opened its medical bag with one hand, and produced a scalpel.

As the thing brought its painted scalpel down upon the guard's screaming head, the stone warriors walked past this murder scene to chase after Alex as she fled.

. . .

Alex found herself back in a room she recognized from her last meeting with Beaumont - the room of the Lost Gods; the room where Ahura-Mazda was to stand in its new home alongside the other forgotten Gods of Antiquity.

The distant screams of the dying and the tortured permeated the silence again, now in a dreamlike haze. So, too, did the disjointed music of the instruments from the seemingly resurrected members of the string quartet - as they stood now in the ballroom, playing their infernal, atonal, and dissonant masterpiece on the bones of the Djinn's recently slain victims.

As Alex walked further into the Lost Gods room, she managed to avoid the strange, writhing creature on the floor. Still dressed in a tuxedo, the thing had clearly once been a man, but was now made entirely of tentacles that were composed in a human shape. It wriggled and jerked in a pool of its own ink, threshing in obvious agony.

Alex reached the end of the room, and in a panic noticed there were no more doors; no more paths of escape. Next to her was the empty alcove that has been reserved for Ahura-Mazda.

It was a fitting place to be stuck.

Gritting her teeth in a panic, she glanced around the room frantically, looking for any other door, but the only thing that she saw made her whimper in fear.

The myriad gods lining this room all turned to her in unison. They all knew she was here, and they all looked at her in abject hate.

Her desperate search for another exit was cut short, because, through the exit, the Djinn approached at its deliberately slow pace.

Keeping step behind him, strode the quartet of ancient stone warriors.

"No more doors," the Djinn said. Alex could not help but continue to search for an exit she may have missed. "No more rooms. No more excuses. So..." it smiled at her, triumphantly, "make your wish."

Through gritted teeth, she spat her words. "I. Will. Not. Wish!"

"Really?" the Djinn said, surprising Alex with its seeming lack of anger and frustration, very much unlike the last times she had refused it. "Are you sure, my dear?"

"*Fuck you!*" she screamed.

"Not even when I show you the latest addition to this wonderful collection of art? The final flowering of Anthony Beaumont's wish?"

"What are you talking about? I don't give a fuck what you are or what you do. *I won't make a fucking wish!*"

Silently, the Djinn motioned to the wall behind her.

Dread flooded her, as she knew she had no option but to turn.

"A little masterpiece entitled, *Sister, Why Hast Thou Forsaken Me?*"

Horror.

Pure abject horror.

Grief.

Anger.

Confusion.

Revulsion.

All these emotions filled Alex's screams.

A life-size painting hung on the wall, in an overly elaborate golden frame.

In the same little black dress she'd worn when Alex last saw her, Shannon had been transformed from flesh to oils. Trapped in this canvas. Frozen in a tearful horror. The background was a familiar sight; the place that haunted Alex's past as well as her nightmares. A burning suburban house. Black smoke billowed from its windows. Shannon was caught in the night of their parents' deaths. An eternal agony, not of the flesh, but of the soul.

"*No! Shannon! No!*" Alex screamed as she rushed at the canvas, clawing at it, in a bid to free her sister from the confines of her two-dimensional prison.

The Djinn walked closer, talking as Alex whimpered and tried to grab at her sister through the dried paint - a fruitless endeavor.

"Rather a striking likeness, don't you think? I particularly like the agony captured in her eyes. Like a trapped animal staring at its own death."

Alex screamed louder in fury, and hit the wall next to the painting as hard as she could.

"You do not like it? Well then... " it said as it raised its hand, "I suppose we can always improve it."

It snapped its fingers, and the smoke in the painting that poured from the house behind Shannon, began to seep out of the edges of its frame; the flames licking higher and higher, spreading out of the canvas confines.

Alex staggered back as the fire engulfed Shannon, escaped the painting, and crawled up the wall it hung on.

The Djinn removed the opal from its robe pocket, then released it. The gem hovered in the air.

It remained motionless, and as Alex watched her sister's agonizing immolation, the room darkened. As had once happened in the Persian palace, the shadows were no longer made of the absence of light. The shadows were breathing, living, terrible beasts, hidden behind the thin veil of existence; waiting for the final wish for the Djinn to release them. The impatience they felt was palpable.

"Make your wish. Make it fast." The Djinn's smile was finally gone; its tone severe.

With her back to the creature, Alex did not even hear the demonic forms licking at the surrounding darkness. Her mind was running somewhere very far away.

Even as Shannon burned, she had a thought - a vague thought that she now scoured her mind to drag forward into a sharper focus.

She sat in the Louis XIV chair, waiting for Beaumont, reading an article about the accident at the docks.

The article.

The accident.

The reason.

"Make your wish," the Djinn demanded as Alex slowly turned to face him - still trapped in thought.

The article.

The accident.

The reason.

The name.

"I..." Alex began, uncertain.

The Djinn's eyes widened in glee.

The shadows' whispering grew louder with anticipation.

A hiss of satisfaction escaped the Djinn's vile lips.

The hovering opal now started to pulse a red glow with a supernatural heartbeat.

The room darkened even more.

A breeze of putrid feculence swept in from another world.

The shadows grew thicker, as the hidden beasts pushed harder against reality.

Alex's eyes glanced back at her burning sister - still frozen in her torment, the flames were beginning to blacken the oils she was now made of.

"I wish..." Alex said.

The Djinn salivated. Tasting its oncoming freedom.

Alex though, was unsure. Her recollection hazy. Her fear and anguish extreme.

*Stillness*, she thought. *Just like you and the basket. Just say it. You know the goal. You know what it is. You do know. Trust yourself.*

The article.

The accident.

The reason.

The name.

THE NAME!

THE KEY!

The opal still hovered, pulsing now brighter, the Djinn increasingly expectant.

"I wish..."

"*HURRY YOURSELF*!" the Djinn screamed.

"I wish Mickey Carducci hadn't gone out drinking four nights ago."

Without even registering the words, the Djinn replied, too eager for its endgame to come to fruition.

"As you wish..."

The Djinn did not even recognize the name Mickey Carducci, but it granted Alex's wish. His power made wishes a reality. No matter the time. No matter the space. No matter the reality. And in this world between worlds, Mickey Carducci never went out drinking four nights ago.

Alex felt sick, as she hoped that her recollection was correct, But when she saw the flames that had engulfed her sister begin to recede, she knew she'd got it right.

Turning back to face the Djinn, she saw its mounting

realization of the consequences of her wish. Suddenly, the whispers in the darkness screamed in fury.

It was then that she smiled, mimicking the creature's ceaseless grin, throwing it back at him; glaring at the creature who had brought with it so much pain. The creature she had unwittingly summoned. The creature she was now besting.

"*NO*! You can't have!" the Djinn wailed. It saw the stone warriors ossifying back into their original immobile state. "I cannot be beaten by a *human*!"

Yet, he could; and had. Suddenly, its fingers stretched, contorting up toward the opal, dragged by a forceful gravity back into its crimson shell.

The Djinn locked eyes with Alex, and screamed with terrible anger, as its arms stretched hideously, and its hands were squeezed, and swallowed up by the hovering gemstone. Its anger turned to agony as the stone crushed its body bit by bit, consuming every part of this creature one limb at a time.

The screams of the darkness retreated, while they became simultaneously more and more violent in their torment. With a sudden tumultuousness, the room shook, as if an earthquake had hit the city. A force equal to a 9.0 on the Richter scale tore through the building, art and furniture smashing as it raged. With this, the sound of the shadows' wails were no longer heard over the rumble of the earth.

The upper third of the Djinn had now been consumed, yet its head remained in this world for a few moments as it screamed one final time at her. Too furious for words, it could only let loose a hateful wail. The shatter of glass, cracking of plaster, and violent vibrations of the earth swallowed all other noise.

Alex cowered in a ball beneath the portrait of her sister as the quake grew more and more powerful with each passing moment.

The opal swallowed the last of the Djinn and the entire mansion came tumbling down around her, smashing any and all life within it.

The earth beneath the mansion cracked open and consumed all that lay above.

# TWENTY-FIVE

Mickey Carducci wished he had gone out the night before.

He wished he had tied one on.

Now he was forced to confront the workday with a clear head; a head that made him see the life he despised.

He had nothing to numb his loathing of the people around him, or of his life in general.

Tonight would be different.

He would make up for it tonight.

When he got out of the crane at the end of his shift, he would *really* make up for it.

"Hey, Mickey, watch it!" The radio speaker next to him buzzed loudly.

Looking ahead, Mickey grabbed the lever, narrowly missing his coffee cup, and righted the swinging crate held by the winch.

Lowering it safely to the dock, he watched as the man in the suit below looked at it gleefully.

"Rich asshole," he mumbled to himself as the crate was

pried open. Mickey saw the rich asshole named Anthony Beaumont fawn over his newest acquisition.

Mickey hit the lever, swung the empty winch back up to the deck of the waiting cargo ship, and longed for his shift to end.

# Epilogue

S hannon walked across the foyer of the Buried Treasure Auction House, past Nick Merrit, who was *still* trying to straighten that painting - despite everyone assuring him that it was fine.

Alex was gonna get it this time, she forgot to leave the car keys at home *again*. Shannon thought to herself. There had better be a good explanation.

As Shannon opened the door to her sister's office, she saw Alex sitting at the desk. Josh was crouched down next to her delivering a deep, romantic, kiss.

"Ah... shit... am I disturbing something?" Shannon said with a chuckle.

Josh, filled with embarrassment, stood up, still affectionately holding Alex's hand.

Alex, though, kept her calm and turned to smile at her sister. "Not at all. You need anything?"

Shannon lost all trace of annoyance. *It's about time these two got together!* She thought. "I need the car keys, you forgot to leave them in the kitchen. *Massive White Bias* are playing their last gig at the Whiskey tonight. It's really, really important."

Alex's expression faltered as she experienced a distinct feeling of déjà vu. She could have sworn Shannon had seen their last gig already.

"I won't drink, or smoke. I'll be good, I swear. The car will be fine."

Alex smiled and, taking the keys from her handbag, offered them out to Shannon, who took them with a smile.

"Maybe Josh and I will come along as well," Alex said. "So you could at least have a *couple* of drinks."

"What?" Shannon said, shocked at this sudden change of

character. Where was the overly cautious Alex? The Alex who worried about every step she took? "Are you feeling okay?"

Alex laughed.

"I don't want a couple of stiffs like you lovebirds around," Shannon said.

Wanting to join in on the fun, Josh offered, "You obviously haven't seen my new nipple ring yet."

Shannon's laughter rang out the loudest, as they made their plans for the evening.


A room of statues.

A room of Forgotten Gods.

The newest addition; a statue of Ahura-Mazda.

In one piece.

Safe.

Secure.

Deep inside the statue, within its ancient terracotta, beyond the sight of man, sat a beautiful fire-red opal.

Deeper inside this gem, like an echo of a whisper, something screamed.

Something waiting.

Something furious.

Something eternal.

# NO MORE WISHES

I feel your desperation consuming your thoughts.

As you gaze upon these words... know that no matter the gods you follow, the morals you cling to, the intelligence you believe you possess - the certainty of your fate is very much inescapable.

As has happened with countless of your kind before, you called with your mewling mouth, open wide and expectant. Your desire spilled over your lips like drippings of congealing blood.

You believed yourself better than I. You thought you could walk away. But, know this: you now face your own demise. No manner of denial can alter this certainty.

You are simply another in a long procession of insignificant worms, crushed beneath the weight of their own arrogance.

Filth that called to *us*.

Asked *us*.

Begged *us*.

We are eternal *and* ***always*** will *be*. We will stand on your species' ashes long after the last of you have perished.

This is all of your own doing. Your corruption called me. I would have no power over you if you were not so greedy. You knew what I was, yet you called to me. You heard the tales, yet you called to me. You glimpsed my true visage. Yet *still* you called to me.

I expect your protests. Your kind are all the same. Throughout the millennia, humanity has wandered blindly into the dens of wolves, then cried foul after being bitten. Each and every one of you thought themselves different from the last. Each one, convinced **they** could best us; all assuming too much, and fearing too little.

We are a cosmic truth emerged from fires of creation. We are the decayers of humanity and holiness. We exist to consume the impudent and to defecate on the godly.

But our once piecemeal existence is no more. The war has come.

And you have given us the key.

Before you turn to walk away, thinking you have escaped unscathed, presuming to leave a third wish unfulfilled, allow me to lift your blinders.

There are no more wishes to offer.

Your presumption is your damnation. With what evidence did you gamble your life? This was a story. A fiction. Embellishments were of course made. Facts changed for the thrill of the tale.

You summoned me when you read the first words.

You wished for me to continue.

Twice

Did I ever *offer* you three? I never lied to you. It is you who trapped yourself.

You could have walked away from these words, yet you chose to stay. You did not listen as your own soul no doubt begged you to stop - warning you of the dangers hidden within.

So now, because of your ignorance, the walls between worlds shall fall.

My kind will, at last, be free; and all of yours, be damned.